LETTERS FROM "J"

LETTERS FROM "J"

The Expanded Life of a Coma Patient

BERNIECE MEAD

Letters from "J"
Copyright © 2010 Berniece Mead

ISBN: 1453623280
ISBN-13: 9781453623282

DEDICATION

This book is dedicated with love and devotion to my very dear friend, Sathya Sai Baba, who came into my life in 1977 and became my Swami. He has been the spiritual director of my heart for lifetimes. He has given me personal direction when things really got tough; when sadness and depression ruled the day, he showed me the light and the way. The reason for the book is Jay, and I also dedicate this creation to this beautiful soul, whom I was blessed to bring into this world some 45 years ago. He has also been my teacher, my friend, and my son. To Swami and to Jay: I love you both with all my heart and soul.

TABLE OF CONTENTS

PREFACE

This book contains our family's experiences resulting from an event in August 1994 that brought our son, Jay Mead, into a coma and instantly changed our life path forever. We never in our wildest thoughts imagined that we would end up receiving an amazing series of communications from him through a medium a few years later. The first letters from Jay came through in the fall of 1997 and have continued sporadically since then.

Upon receiving the first few letters, we shared them only with close friends and family whom we felt would be understanding and open-minded. Then, within a few months, I decided to go out on a limb and share them with other family members at Thanksgiving time. I wasn't sure at all how they would be received by some of the family, but their response was surprising. Without exception, not only were people touched emotionally by the letters, they were also deeply affected by the content and grateful to have "heard" from Jay in this way.

Although I had my doubts about how this communication could take place at all, I could not deny that the letters sounded very authentic. The messages sounded "just like Jay" and always contained references and phrases that Debbie, the "scribe" or medium—who lived over 400 miles away and had not known us before—could not have possibly known. Even more convincing, on an inner level the letters rang true, and they contained intriguing, powerful, and often challenging insights into Jay's new world—and ours. They were filled with spiritual advice that was extremely compelling.

My volunteer work with the Sri Sathya Sai Baba organization—a spiritual education and service organization—keeps me traveling to all parts of the country, conducting teacher trainings and speaking at retreats and other events, besides international travel for similar events. I began sharing some of Jay's first letters with a few people as I traveled. The reaction was consistent: they had no problem at all believing that the letters came from Jay. My doubts began to lessen slightly, and as we received more letters, I would share them with a few of my close friends, and they would become excited and express to me that I had to share these letters with others. Many told me that I needed to think about writing a book, to share not only Jay's letters but also our family's experiences with Sri Sathya Sai Baba, the holy man of whom we had already been followers for seventeen years at the time Jay entered the coma in 1994. But I had deep reservations about writing a book.

Starting in the very first letter, Jay also mentioned my writing a book and continued to prompt me in this direction over the years in other letters, but I still found it difficult to contemplate opening my heart and sharing in print the very personal aspects of these experiences. Partly, I felt reluctant to re-open the traumatic emotions surrounding Jay's experience, and of reliving the grief by writing about the events. On the other hand, I had continued sharing Jay's letters in talks and had always received a wonderful response. A medical doctor once approached me after a workshop in Connecticut, saying that it was very important that I share the messages in Jay's letters, because people in the medical field needed to know there is more to coma patients than it appears by their outer status and expression. This doctor had worked with coma patients, so she was in a position to assess the general lack of understanding in the medical field on this subject.

So for many years, I sat on the fence, still feeling reluctant to write this story. But then the body of letters kept growing steadily, and the messages continued to be so full of spiritual insights. From time to time I would read some of the latest letters at speaking engagements and would continue to receive requests and encouragement to put the letters in book form. People seemed to get immediate "take-aways" from hearing the information—inspirational gems they could easily relate to and put to use in their lives, and which would move them to another level in their spiritual understanding. Jay's messages touched people's hearts.

What Jay had to say about his own experience and that of other coma patients was both revealing and astounding. How could we have known, based on their outer physical appearance, that coma patients' have a *life* that is so rich, complex, active, and free.

So, when presented with a rare and unexpected opportunity in July 2008 to speak directly with Sai Baba, I asked him if I should share the letters we had received from Jay. He told me repeatedly to "share"—"share the letters." Probably this instruction, more than anything else, tipped the scales for me, for Baba undoubtedly knew that I would not have ventured ahead on any such "out of the ordinary" project without his express approval.

So, I decided to go ahead and let the chips fall where they may. Only my ego could suffer anyway—which I felt needed to get out of the way and let truth prevail. I figured, for the most part, only those who were interested in the subject would read the book anyway, and if such a book could help to raise the level of awareness in others, then it would be worth the love, persistence, and energy that it took to finish the task.

This book contains the story of Jay's "transitional experience," upon which he entered the coma state, and our family's journey leading up to and throughout this experience. It contains seventeen letters from "J"—some of which are quite lengthy. These were all received over a twelve-year period, between October 9, 1997, and July 27, 2009.

All of Jay's letters have been spontaneous and irregular, sometimes with many years between them. We have never asked Debbie to contact Jay, thinking it best just to let these communications happen in God's and Jay's timing, not through our prompting.

—Berniece Mead
August 2010

ACKNOWLEDGMENTS

To all of my friends, who have encouraged me for the last ten years to write this book of Jay's letters, a big thanks. Without your love and total support I could not have succeeded in completing the manuscript.

To my good friend, Carole Tapp, who put so much energy into the book and was very excited about publishing the book through her publishing company in Oklahoma City, Legendary Publishing. However, as sometimes things happen to change the course, Carole died in a traffic accident July 28, 2009. When I received the news from her husband, Barry, I was with Jay. I began to cry, while Jay had a big smile on his face. I knew that Jay knew on some level that Carole was all right and had completed her tasks on earth on time.

To Dr. Mike Congleton and his wife, Carol, for gifting me with speech recognition software, and to Pravin Wagh for installing the program on the computer. It's fun to speak into a microphone and watch the words appear on the screen.

To Corinn Codye, who has been my editing supervisor since the Sai Spiritual Education Teacher's Manual written in 1995. *Letters from J* would not be so readable if it were not for her meticulous editing. She knew when I needed to say more and when I needed to say less. Her guidance was invaluable to someone who could speak but not write well. Thank you, Corinn, for all your love and support, and for making this book a work of art from the heart.

To Laila Nabulsi, who used her eye for art in combo with her heart to help design the cover, and to Jan Mead for the photo of Jay and me that appears on the back cover.

And to Jay's dear friend, Kimberly Sickel, who added her expertise as a graphic designer, to organize the final format in placing the pictures in proper sequence and making the book look good and reader friendly.

Last but certainly not least, to Debbie Imhoff, who came into this particular drama in 1997 when I asked her, after learning of her talents in this area, if she might be able to communicate with Jay. In her humbleness and sweetness, she simply said, "I don't know; we'll try." She succeeded in connecting with his mind, and two weeks later the letters began to come from Jay through this wonderful channel. Even though she has faced some serious challenges throughout these past years, she always kept her communication with Jay open and free. Jay loves you, and so do we, Debbie. Thank you! Thank you!

LETTERS FROM "J"

CHAPTER 1

OUR FAMILY

Our son, Jay Ronald Mead, was born on July 26, 1965, and his sister, Jan Eileen, on November 7, 1968. My husband, Ron, and I were young teachers at the time, working in the public schools in Southern California. In a way, Jay's birth, for me, marked the beginning of a personal search for spiritual answers, because I suffered greatly from a lengthy post-partum depression and started questioning everything—why bring a child into a world filled with strife and sorrow, what is the meaning of life, and so on. Although I was active in a conservative Christian church, it did not seem to provide the answers I was looking for. When I came across the work of Edgar Cayce and learned about reincarnation, I started to feel as if I were finding some truths, and I kept exploring in this direction.

Jay and Jan Mead (1972)

Eventually, in 1977, Ron and I learned about Sri Sathya Sai Baba of India, and we were especially draw to his teachings, such as:

All religions are pathways to God.
There is only one God, and he is omnipresent; there is only one religion, the religion of love.
The essence of all religions is 'Love all, serve all,' and 'Help ever, hurt never.'

About five months after we first heard of Sri Sathya Sai Baba, we attended a public meeting of the Sathya Sai Baba Society in Orange County. Several individuals had just returned from India and were telling their stories. We met Elsie Cowan, whose husband, Walter, had been raised from the dead by Sai Baba, in India, during December 1971. It was wonderful to hear all these stories, and there we also learned about a weekly get-together at someone's home in Buena Park. A new spiritual direction was rapidly coming together for us, and we were extremely happy about it. Furthermore, the people who had just returned from India told us that Sai Baba had instructed them to come home and start children's spiritual education classes. Ron and I knew immediately that this role was where we belonged, because we were both professional schoolteachers and had children of our own, ages nine and twelve.

The children's program at that time was called by the Sanskrit name, Bal Vikas, meaning "the blossoming of the child," or in a broader sense, education that results in "the blossoming of human excellence." In the beginning the Bal Vikas program centered mostly on the unity of faiths and teaching the children to meditate. Later, the classes were based on Sai Baba's teachings on developing virtuous character and morality through the "five human values" (truth, right action, peace, love, and nonviolence).

Within a few months, I began teaching these Bal Vikas classes in my home, starting with five children, including Jay and Jan. At some point, I began teaching the children the "light meditation"—as taught by Sai Baba.[1] Right away, Jay had a very personal and vivid inner experience of Sai Baba. Jay had recently acquired a small 110 camera that he used to take pictures with. The very first time he engaged in the guided visualization of the light, Baba appeared to him in the visualization—came to him right out of the flame—and took a picture of Jay with a small 110 camera, identical to Jay's. Then Baba walked back into the flame.

---

1 In the "light meditation" taught by Sai Baba, one visualizes a flame of light in the heart, spreading that light to all parts of the body—the tongue, the mind, the hands and feet, that all these instruments of thought, word, and action would be influenced by the light, to do only good—and then expanding the light outward, infinitely, to include everyone and everything.

Jay, however, did not even mention this remarkable experience until several days later at dinner. I asked him, "Why didn't you share this with the class?" He had been very happy about the experience but did not consider it a big deal, saying, as if he had not been surprised at all, "That's what Baba does!"

Simultaneous with the Bal Vikas classes, we also continued attending Christian churches, searching for one that fit, because Baba also taught, "I'm not here to start a new religion. Don't leave your religion to follow me, but become a better Christian, Buddhist, Hindu, or Muslim."

Accordingly, I wanted the children to continue going to Sunday school, so they did, and they experienced no confusion or misunderstanding about doing both. However, when Jay decided to be baptized after attending a summer camp with his Sunday school teacher, Jay told his teacher about Sai Baba, and the teacher had nothing good to say about it. Jay felt shocked that his Sunday school teacher didn't even want to hear about our "other" spiritual life.

Jay remained in the Bal Vikas class until he was eighteen, and Jan until she was sixteen, after which she joined a Church of Religious Science[2]

---

2 Church of Religious Science congregations are now called by the name, "Center(s) for Spiritual Living."

youth group. This group was more open-minded about Sai Baba; many of the members had even gone to India to receive Sai Baba's darshan.[3] We eventually left off attending the Christian church, and Ron and I poured all our energy into the Sri Sathya Sai Baba organization. Over the next few years, we hosted occasional "fifth Sunday meetings" in our large home in Fountain Valley. These meetings gave all the Sai Baba centers in Los Angeles and Orange Counties a chance to meet together. We also opened our home for other meetings and teacher trainings, because we had a huge room upstairs that was perfect for such events.

One time, Jack Hislop[4] came to visit the children's classes at our home; he brought his famous cross—a small wooden cross that Sai Baba had manifested for him, which Baba said he had reconstituted of atoms from the wood of the original cross of Jesus. Hislop let the children hold this cross.

---

3 *darshan*, the opportunity or blessing of seeing a holy being; seeing divinity.
4 Dr. John S. Hislop, author of several well-known books about Sri Sathya Sai Baba (*Conversations with Sathya Sai Baba*, 1978; *My Baba and I*, 1985; *Seeking Divinity*, 1997 post.) and first USA Sai organization president.

TRIPS TO INDIA

Sai Baba's main ashram is called Prasanthi Nilayam, meaning "Abode of Highest Peace," located in the village of Puttaparthi, about 55 miles (90 kilometers) northeast of Bangalore, in southern India. Sai Baba was born in this remote, rural village in 1926.

I first traveled to India to see Sri Sathya Sai Baba during the summer of 1978, about a year and a half after we first heard about him. It was a remarkable pilgrimage that confirmed for me Baba's omniscience, omnipresence, and omnipotence. The many stories of my personal journey and lessons learned at the feet of Sri Sathya Sai Baba since 1977 could easily fill another book, but I will focus here only on those experiences that have most closely to do with Jay's story.

The very next year, in the summer of 1979, I was fortunate to go on a second trip to Sai Baba's ashram, along with another lady. During that trip, Baba called seven of us for an interview. Once he had seated us in the interview room, he made us vibhuti right from his hands and started speaking to us in English. He began talking about my family and mentioned my husband and son. Jay was having some problems in school with dyslexia.

Baba talked to me about Jay's problems and said, "I will help him."

After this summertime trip, Ron and I returned to our respective schools as teachers, and the children as students. Jay was in junior high, attending the same school where his dad taught science and math. Jay had dyslexia and was having some trouble with math, but he couldn't get into special classes because his IQ was too high. Unexpectedly, the school psychologist approached Ron one day and said, "Although Jay doesn't really qualify, I'm going to put him in a special class. I know it will help him." Then he said rather ruefully, "I don't know why I'm doing this."

Ron and I had a good laugh over this, because we knew why it was happening. We recognized the signs of the omnipresent Sai at work in our lives, fulfilling his word. Baba had said he would help Jay, and he was. Jay finished his school year successfully.

The following summer, in 1980, Ron and Jay went to India together while Jan and I stayed home. Jan and I would take our turn the following summer. The boys had a good trip. In those days you were even permitted to take a camera into darshan, and they were able to take some wonderful pictures. Jay, however, became very ill while there, and it was his dad who nursed him back to health. They didn't call Jan and I—that was years before the Internet and cell phone service—so we heard nothing from them until another friend came home bearing a letter from Jay and Ron and gave us a telephone call, telling us how sick Jay had been.

In 1982 we decided to go as a family and take both the children to India. By now Jay and Jan were in high school, and we decided this trip would take place at a critical point in their development. Besides, we definitely felt we were "being called" to go. When it comes to traveling to see Sai Baba, sometimes it feels as if the decision is not even yours to make; events and circumstances can carry you there, seeming like nothing else could possibly happen at that time. This trip, not only did we wish to go—because we felt we might not ever again get the same chance to go as a family, with the children moving on in their teen years—but also, as soon as we decided to go, several other families decided to go too, and pretty soon we were a group of seventeen in all. We were swept up together in this wave, and the travel plans came together smoothly. A similar thing can happen in reverse, if the timing and circumstances are not right to go on such a trip. No matter your efforts, the plans will fall through.

We experienced many blessings that trip. We were able to take some good photographs, and Baba stopped right in front of Jan and made vibhuti[5] for her one day during darshan. When darshan took place, usually Sai Baba would come out and walk near the rows of people who were seated, mostly on the ground, waiting for this chance to see him and possibly interact with him. With whom Baba decides to interact is entirely his will and totally unpredictable. As he passed by, Jan, who was sitting on the front row, asked Baba for an interview for our family, and he turned around and smiled at her. Then, with a circular wave of his hand, he made vibhuti, the sacred ash, and poured it into her hands, and into those of a friend sitting next to her. Jan was ecstatic with this experience.

In those years inside the ashram, there used to be a little beverage stand at the end of a line of shopping stalls near the darshan grounds. The children would go to this "pop shop" every day. One day, before going to get a soda, Jay said, "I'd like to have a chocolate milkshake."

---

5 *Vibhuti* is sacred ash often materialized by Sai Baba, symbolizing, among other things, the splendor and glory of God that emanates as unending streams of blessings and grace.

I said, "Dream on, son! There's no way you'll get a milkshake here; they don't even have ice cream."

To my surprise, the next thing I knew, Jay and Jan came in the door, each sucking on a chocolate milkshake. I said to Jay, "Where did you get that?"

Jay answered, "I got it at the pop shop." Then he continued, with a broad smile on his face, "The attendant asked us if we'd like a chocolate milkshake. He said they had just received some from Bangalore. I figured Baba had the milkshakes ordered just for us!"

The next day, Jay and Jan decided they'd like another chocolate milkshake, so they went to the pop shop and asked for one. The attendant looked at Jay with surprise and said, "Son, we don't have chocolate milkshakes."

Jay said, "Well, I got one here yesterday."

The attendant just shook his head and said sternly, "You've never gotten a milkshake here, because we've never had them!"

This is what we call a *leela* (divine sport or play, divine prank) of the Lord. He had given the children their heart's desire; it had made them happy, and they were grateful. It was a sweet *leela*—literally!

Baba continued to be attentive and sweet to our family in the darshan line. With smiles, he'd take our letters. Jay celebrated his seventeenth birthday while we were there. On that day, Jay bought a garland of flowers to offer to Sai Baba, and Baba accepted it when he came. Again, there are no guarantees that Baba will even look at you or come near you, much less accept a letter or offering from you. That he blessed us in these many ways made us all very happy.

Sai Baba approaches Jay on his 17th birthday (July 26, 1982)

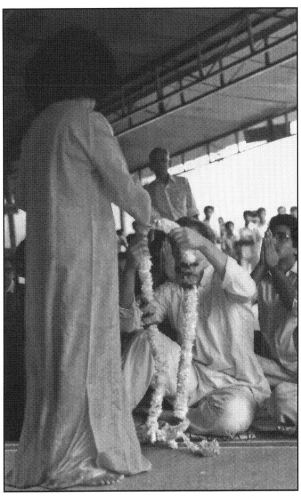

Baba accepts a garland from Jay

The trip was a good one for our family, even though I experienced some painful feelings of disappointment that we didn't get an interview with Sai Baba. That was part of my lessons of detachment to learn. But in retrospect, through the interactions that Baba gave Jay and Jan, perhaps he answered Ron's and my prayers after all, just in a different—and possibly better—form than we imagined and desired. Sai tells us, "I do not make mistakes."[6]

---

6 *Sathya Sai Speaks* (SSS) 30:31, end quote following discourse of Nov. 22, 1997.

Sometimes, even if you have hunger, God does not give you food—just to keep you in check and in control. . . . There is a proper time and the proper way, for your own sake. Even a spiritual experience—sometimes God withholds it, because God does everything for man's good.

—Sri Sathya Sai Baba[7]

---

7 In Hislop, John, *Conversations with Sathya Sai Baba* (Sri Sathya Sai Baba Society of America, publ. by Birth Day Publishing, San Diego, California, 1978), p. 9.

CHAPTER 2

JAY'S TALENT

As an adult, Jay was an actor—a stage performer and stunt man. In hindsight, I can look back and pick out a few incidents that took place during Jay's school years that gave clues to the direction of his talents. When Jay was in seventh grade, one of the teachers asked the students to get up and give an impromptu speech. No one else volunteered, but Jay got right up and launched right into a spiel that had everyone laughing in no time. The teacher was amazed and talked to us later about it; he couldn't believe how entertaining Jay had been.

Then, in high school, Jay wrote an English paper describing the experiencing of getting his first traffic ticket. His flair for the dramatic came out in his sensory descriptions: he went into minute detail about looking at the approaching officer in the rearview mirror, the squeaking of his boots as he approached, and so on.

Also during his high school years, Jay developed an interest in theatre and acting. Although Jay sang in the choir, we had no clue that he had any talent or interest in theatre, but it surfaced big time during his sophomore year. He had a friend who was involved in the school drama productions, who planned to try out for a part in the student production of the musical, *West Side Story*. This friend suggested that Jay also try out, and Jay studied the scene, memorized the lines, and auditioned for the part of the character named "Action." He didn't get the part.

But then, unexpectedly, the boy who had landed the part took a job and couldn't participate in the musical, so Jay got a chance to audition again for the part, and this time he landed it. I remember sitting in the audience during the play and being blown away, because he was absolutely superb. He put his whole heart into the character. "Action" was supposed to be a very excitable and easily-angered gang member, and Jay was completely believable. One of his teachers played the part of "Officer Krupke," and he told Jay afterward, "When you came at me with that anger, I felt it. You actually scared me!"

West Side Story is based on the Shakespeare tragedy, *Romeo and Juliet*, and ironically, the Romeo and Juliet theme has surfaced in different ways in Jay's life. When he was just a little boy, eight or nine years old, he had a cassette tape of Tchaikovsky's "Romeo and Juliet," a classical symphonic piece written in the late 1800s. Jay played that tape over and over and over again. He just *loved* it and couldn't seem to get enough of it. He even took it on a camping trip with us, sitting in the right-hand front seat of our motor home, playing it incessantly on the tape player. Somehow that music really spoke to him.

Then, as a teen, he had his first acting experiences in *West Side Story*, which is but the story of "Romeo and Juliet" in a more contemporary setting. The plot involves some tragic events that cut off some lives in the prime of youth, and one could even draw a parallel here, based on the events later that resulted in Jay entering a long-lasting coma when he was in his twenties.

After *West Side Story*, now that Jay was "in" with the drama program, he kept going with enthusiasm. He participated in all the theatre productions for the rest of his high school years—including the musicals *Guys and Dolls* and *The Music Man*. Jay loved Shakespeare and played in such productions as *Twelfth Night* and *A Midsummer Night's Dream* in high school and college. After high school, he took drama classes at Golden West and Orange Coast community colleges.

While still a senior in high school, Jay got a job working as a cook and dishwasher in the employee lounge at Knott's Berry Farm, a major Southern California theme park in Buena Park, not far from where we lived. Knott's Berry Farm has an Old West theme, based on the original Calico Ghost Town. The main square has the look of an old western town from the late 1800s, and a narrow gauge steam locomotive train ride circles the park and comes through the main square. Other attractions include a stagecoach ride, a water tower, a gold mine, a saloon and dance hall, and various other typical Old West buildings.

Groups of actors, dressed in cowboy garb, stage entertaining fake fights and "gun battles"—the "good guys" vs. the "bad guys"—such as train robbers or cattle rustlers battling it out with a sheriff and his posse. The theme park also featured daily main stage shows starring a stunt team and their comedy routines.

Jay was thrilled with these shows and very soon began riding the train, watching the actors who staged a "robbery" during the train ride. He memorized all their lines and moves—for all the characters. Jay was very quick at memorizing. He then went to the management and asked if he could audition as an actor in the train robbery, but they didn't have any openings.

Acting in the Knott's shows was not easy to break into, as struggling young actors tended to hold onto such steady, paying gigs, once they landed them. The manager explained the situation to Jay and put it very bluntly, "Son, someone's going to have to die for you to get onto the acting team."

I doubt if the manager was trying to be prophetic, but again, Jay's career path must have been in the stars, because, uncannily, it wasn't two weeks later that one of the actors actually had a heart attack and passed away. Jay attended the funeral and met the other actors from the train robbery. When they held an audition, Jay tried out and got into the train robbery team at Knott's, and that's how his professional career as an actor and stunt performer got started.

Then Jay started watching the main stage shows, the stunt revues. He adopted the same strategy as for getting into the cast of the train robbery, which was to memorize all the parts in the show. He tried out at the next audition, and it didn't take him long to get on the stunt team. He did all this part time, while attending Orange Coast College. After two years in college, he left school and worked full time at Knott's. He considered finishing a degree in drama but could see that he was already ahead of most theatre graduates fresh out of college, in terms of his career. On-the-job training, high motivation, and natural talent had given him the skills for the job.

Meanwhile, both Jay and Jan moved out of their teens. In May 1988, at age nineteen, Jan got married; we gave her our blessings and a large wedding. Our first grandchild, Nathan, was born the following year. Also in 1989, I took an early retirement from the public school system. The next year, in April 1990, Jay married Paula, a fellow aspiring actor at Knott's Berry Farm; he met her when she was working in the "Calico Saloon."

In his stage and stunt work, Jay quickly established himself as a wonderful actor and stand-up comic, and an able stunt performer. He and the other actors were like a family, in this highly physical, athletic, show business career. Stunt performers in movies may double for actors, but they don't usually handle speaking parts. These live stage shows required it all—the ability to draw in the crowd, keep them laughing, surprise them, and astound them with the physical falls and fights. Jay entertained and brought laughter to thousands and thousands of visitors at Knott's Berry Farm.

Jay Mead (front row, third from right) and stunt team
members posing in front of the steam locomotive
at Knott's Berry Farm (circa 1990).

Jay would describe his job as "like playing cowboys and Indians all day long." When they weren't performing, they were training and practicing. He learned the profession of stunt work from the existing stunt team, who trained all the new cast members in all their physical moves.

Jay eventually became good enough to train others. He bought a video camera and used it as a teaching tool. He would film people doing their practice stunts, and then they would review the videotape, with Jay pointing out what changes were needed to improve the stunts' effectiveness and safety. By playing back these tapes in slow motion, the actors could analyze and hone their movements.

It wasn't too long before one of Jay's fellow actors at Knott's began working at Universal Studios in a Wild West stunt show; this friend thought a lot of Jay's talents not only as an actor but as a trainer of the stunt team, and he recommended that the people at Universal try to get Jay involved too. This led to Jay working steadily in the stage shows at both places, Universal Studios as well as Knott's. Jay kept developing his acting career and also branched out into some work on TV ("The Young and the Restless"), movies (some B-rated karate films marketed in Japan), and commercials (Polaroid cameras). As such, he was a member of the Screen Actors Guild. He was also a regular cast member of the Murder Mystery Dinner Theater in Long Beach, California. One time he went with this troupe on a cruise where their murder-mystery production was part of the entertainment.

Also, he worked various weekends at the original Calico Ghost Town out in the Mojave Desert near Barstow, California. Over a hundred years ago, Calico had been an authentic ghost town—a silver, borax, and gold mining center, before it died out in 1907. Walter Knott, the founder of Knott's Berry Farm, had preserved this historic town and later donated it to the County of San Bernardino, California. The entertainment at Calico included mock gunfights and living history characters.

Jay during one of his high fall stunts (circa 1992)

JAY'S WAYS

I am sure every mother has at least a few treasured memories of her children when they were young. When Jay was eight years old, he made me a Mother's Day card and cooked breakfast for me and for his grandmother, who was living with us at the time. On this card was a picture of a mother bird sitting on an upper limb of a tree, holding a worm in her beak. Underneath her he had drawn a nest with three baby birds; they had their beaks up in the air, waiting for their mother to feed them. Jay had written a caption under this drawing: "What would the world do without mothers?" This sweet observation so touched my heart.

If I had to summarize what Jay was like as a person, I would have to say that he loved to tease. This could be fun, but it probably drove his sister, for one, crazy at times. He was a jokester, through and through. With Jay, a conversation could not seem to get serious for long, as he would usually throw in something off the wall or turn it in a silly direction. According to his sister, Jan, he loved the television show, *The Three Stooges*, and had memorized a lot of their routines, especially those of "Curly" (the original one). The "Curly" influence was identifiable in many of Jay's performances.

Jay was also generous with his time and talent. When I was still teaching school, besides teaching kindergarten, I taught the school choir and put on plays involving the children. Jay was a great help to me in these drama productions; he would help me with blocking out the players' positions and movements, and he was great with the children. They loved him. One day, the "Early Show" on one of the Los Angeles television networks went out to Calico Ghost Town in the desert and filmed a show that Jay performed in. The morning it aired, I turned the program on for my class so we could all watch it together. The children loved it, of course, and the next time Jay came to the school, he was a big celebrity.

Jay always had a lot of empathy for people. One time after he got married, a fellow he knew was planning to give himself a birthday party. This fellow was not very well liked by Jay's other friends. That same day, I had invited Jay home for one of his favorite dinners—fried okra and other down-home dishes, since Paula was working evenings at that time. But Jay declined, saying that if he didn't go to this friend's birthday party, he was afraid no one else would show up.

Jay never wanted to hurt anyone; he would never have caused anyone any harm intentionally, and to my knowledge, Jay never got into any fights or squabbles. People often sought him out for advice, and he was more likely to bring people together and smooth things out with laughter, than to cause friction.

Jay, being in a career that demanded a lot of physical strength and agility, kept himself in good shape. He worked out regularly at the gym and had a brown belt in karate. He was working on his black belt; his wife already had one. He also loved ocean diving and was a certified scuba diver. He would say to me, "I've gotta go visit them thar' little fishies—see my little friends today," and he and a friend would go off diving somewhere along the Orange County coast. He loved fish and maintained a salt-water aquarium at home. Salt-water habitats are delicate set-ups that take a lot of monitoring, and he took care of those fish just like babies. One of his fish was a goofy eel that responded to Jay enough to peek out around a rock whenever Jay looked in the tank. One day that eel, almost a foot long, jumped out of the tank, and I found it on the floor, nearly done in.

Jay got a big kick out of visiting the Oklahoma farm area where Ron and I grew up and where we still had family. In the fall, during the cotton harvest, Jay would get up on the truck where the cotton was being piled as it was harvested. One of the farm jobs was to "stomp down" the cotton, so more could fit in the truck bed. Jay turned this chore into a comedy show, using his stunt routines to entertain the cousins, by jumping and falling into the heaps of cotton.

This photo shows Jay's humorous side (circa 1992).

DOWN-SIZING

By the end of 1993, Jan and her husband had moved in with us, saving money to buy a house, and they had another baby, Nicholas, born in May of that year. Nathan was by then four years old and very fond of his Uncle Jay and the fun times they had together, before Jan and her family moved to Kansas in January 1994.

Jay and his wife, meanwhile, were settled and living well. Their acting careers were developing, and they appeared to be enjoying life while making long-range plans to start a family after a couple of years.

The year 1994 marked a lot of rapid life changes for Ron and I. But we could not imagine, going into that year, the immensity of the changes in store for us later that summer. In 1993, I had been appointed National Education Coordinator for the USA Sri Sathya Sai Baba organization. My duties would include traveling and training teachers all over the country for the *Bal Vikas*[8] or Sai Spiritual Education (SSE) program. All of a sudden, taking care of a large house just didn't seem to make

---

8 *Bal Vikas* translates as "the blossoming of the child," or in a broader sense, education that results in "the blossoming of human excellence," through developing virtuous character and morality through the "five human values" of truth, right action, peace, love, and nonviolence.

sense for Ron and me any more, especially since Jay and Jan were well established in their own households. So, we decided to sell our big house in Fountain Valley, California, and downscale our way of living.

Ron and I purchased a new motor home—a recreational vehicle (RV), and we made plans to travel the USA while I conducted teacher trainings. We figured it would take us about a year to visit all the Bal Vikas classes around the country. Along the way, we looked forward to visiting scenic and historic parts of our motherland. We thought we might settle eventually in a small house, probably in our birth state, Oklahoma, on or near one of its beautiful lakes. Real estate was much more affordable in Oklahoma than in California, and we figured that from the middle of the country I could easily fly more easily in any direction to conduct teacher trainings.

We were successful in selling our house by April 1994 and had to be moved out by the end of June. Finally, the house was empty, and everything gone or packed. The last evening we sat on the floor and talked about our new way of life, which was about to begin.

Jay came by for a farewell visit to the house. He went one-by-one to every room, thanking each one for what it had meant to him and for all the memories of times past. I just couldn't do that; I found it much too painful. I shed a few tears as we walked out of the house for the last time, turned around for one last look, said our goodbyes, and kept moving.

∞

Attachment presents a never-ending attraction toward objects. But it is very easy to renounce! Simply think, "Everything belongs to God. Nothing is mine!" This is the way to transcend attachment. . . . You can say, "My home, my land, my wife, my child, my wealth, my car, and so on, but bear this in mind: all these things are for use only, not for ownership. They are God's property. You must part with everything at death. . . . So, gradually decrease the idea of "mine." . . . Experience the world with your power of discrimination. . . . Use the world to engage in constructive actions, to walk the path of truth.

—Sri Sathya Sai Baba[9]

9 *Summer Showers in Brindavan 1995*, ch. 9, pp. 157-159.

CHAPTER 3

THE LIFE-CHANGING EVENT

Our first trip in the new motor home was to Oklahoma to establish in-state residence by opening a post office box in Carnegie, where Ron and I were from originally and where Ron's parents still lived. We bought a new Saturn car to pull behind the motor home, registered both vehicles in Oklahoma, and delivered Ron's pickup truck to Jan and her husband in Kansas. After visiting with them for a few days, we went on to visit family members. Along the way, we picked up my niece, Kathy, who was to come back to California with us for the summer and also go along with me on a trip to India in August.

On the way home, Ron did most of the driving, and Kathy and I just enjoyed the scenery. In an RV, you are able to get up and walk around, even get something out of the refrigerator if you like. I was doing a lot of research for developing a new *Sai Spiritual Education Teacher's Manual*, to be used in SSE teacher trainings. I needed to locate a great many quotes from Sai Baba's discourses and writings, to underpin the curriculum and teaching methods, and one day as we were driving down the road in Arizona, I came across a passage in *Sathya Sai Speaks, Volume 10,*[10] that really disturbed me, and I couldn't get it out of my mind.

> *Egoism is a thorny bush, for which, when planted and fostered in one's heart, one has to pay the penalty. Egoism makes enemies of fast friends and ruins many good causes and projects, for it does not allow two good men to work together. Grief follows it like a shadow.*
>
> *But where there is no ego—joy, peace, courage, cooperation, and love flourish. When man is aware that the same divine consciousness that motivates him is that which*

10 *Sathya Sai Speaks* is an ongoing series, a collection of Sai Baba's public discourses, with a new volume published each year or so, compiling his talks from the time he first began giving discourses in 1953. Volume 10 contains his discourses from 1970.

equally motivates all others, then love drives the ego into the background and takes charge of man's activities, words, and thoughts.

Consider this incident: a man suddenly loses his son and is in great grief. So a neighbor goes to him and tries to console and comfort him by various arguments and anecdotes. "My dear friend! Why is a man born? Why does he die? The reason for his birth also explains his death. Birth means death. Fate plays strange games with us. We are but puppets in the show. What is the good of grieving over the dead?" He pours all the Vedanta (wisdom of the Upanishads; spiritual wisdom) he knows into the ears of the bereaved person. But the grief continues as before, until the man, unaided, becomes aware of the truth himself.

A few months later, the neighbor loses his son. Now the man who received all the Vedanta a few months ago comes to him and repeats the same quotations in succession. He says that one lives only as long as one's karma (results of past action) lasts, and that one's life is cut short when one has no more karma to atone for. [This cycle of birth and death] is all a question of paying off old debts.

But these statements do not console the aggrieved neighbor, for he feels the loss as entirely his. When ego is awake, no wisdom can appeal. The feeling, "my son," is the root cause of one person's grief and another's calm.

— Sri Sathya Sai Baba[11]

11 *Sathya Sai Speaks*, 14:12, Oct. 11, 1978.

As soon as I read this message, I thought, "What if I lost my son?" and the thought would not leave me. I felt deep distress just touching upon the thought. I quickly turned the page and began reading the rest of the discourse.

I had a deep attachment to my son, Jay, which had started even before he was born. While student teaching years before, I had met a little boy child by the name of Jay. He was very cute and sweet, and I had thought to myself, "One day I will have a Jay of my own." Two years later I married Ron, and two years later I had Jay and became immediately very attached to him, which caused me no end of worries about his well-being.

The discourse went on about ego being the root cause of one's attachment and grief, and getting rid of the sense of "me" and "mine." I could not seem to shake the sad feelings this passage brought up in me.

We arrived in California on Thursday, and on Friday evening went to my sister Eileen's in Torrance and spent the night there before going on to Ojai, a beautiful village-like town east of Santa Barbara, California. This visit was for the purpose of working on the *Sai Spiritual Education Teacher's Manual* with Mrs. Pat Wing, another very experienced *Bal Vikas* teacher. Ron and I planned to stay at a nice campground at Casitas Lake, near Ojai.

That Friday evening, Jay came by my sister's place in Torrance after work at Universal Studios. He looked quite tired, so I suggested to him, "Why don't you take the weekend off and come with us up to Ojai?"

Rather solemnly, he said, "Mom, I can't do that. This is summertime, our busiest season. I need to work." He was working at Knott's Berry Farm for the weekend, which meant he would have fewer speaking parts and more stunts to perform, such as high falls.

Jay not only acted in the skits, he had been the head of the stunt team at the park and had trained the other actors. They were a close-knit group. He was known as a stickler for training and safety, very meticulous in his work.

When I hugged Jay goodbye that evening, I felt a little sadness, and he had a pensive look as we said our goodbyes. As fate would have it, these were the last words I would hear from him for a very long time.

Another of Jay's professional photos (circa 1992).

THE NEWS ARRIVES

That Saturday afternoon, while Pat Wing and I were busy working on the teacher's manual, we received a call from Ron, who was still at the campground. He had been visited by a California Highway Patrol (CHP) officer. Although Jay knew where we were, his wife didn't know the name of the campground, so she had called the Highway Patrol to locate us in Ojai.

The officer had given Ron the news that Jay had been injured at work and was in surgery at the University of California, Irvine (UCI) Medical Center. The CHP officer suggested that we get to the hospital as soon as we could. Ron asked if the message meant that Jay had died. The officer answered that this was not the case—Jay was still in surgery. The UCI hospital is located near the Interstate-5 freeway in the City of Orange, a couple of hours south of Ojai.

I left immediately to return to our campsite. Ron and my niece, Kathy, had everything ready, so we could leave as soon as I arrived. My mind was topsy-turvy at this news, and my emotions in a tailspin. My thoughts kept returning to the passage of Sai Baba's that I had read three days earlier.

"Lord, are you taking our son away from us?" I kept asking. "Please help me to have some peace with this and to accept whatever happens." I was trying my best to reduce my feelings of worry and attachment, and to build up a feeling of acceptance of God's will. But my heart was full of grief and my mind numb.

It was a beautiful Saturday evening, and the moon was full as it rose over the hills surrounding the Ventura area. The traffic moved at an unusually steady pace, especially for the greater Los Angeles area, which we had to cross. The three of us did little talking; we just kept repeating the Divine Name, each of us dealing with our own shock, sadness, and sense of uncertainty. Kathy and Jay had been close as cousins growing up, and this was difficult for her too.

Jay's wife, Paula, met us in the reception room of the hospital; several of the guys from the stunt team at Knott's Berry Farm were also there. Jay had come out of surgery by then. He was on the critical list and still in the recovery room, so we could not see him for several hours. Jay had gone into a coma instantly upon falling and has never regained full waking consciousness, as the medical world would describe it. Paula, Kathy, Ron, and I went into a little waiting room and began chanting the Gayatri mantra quietly:

> *Om bhur bhuvah suvaha, Tat savitur varenyam*
>
> *Bhargo devasya dhimahi, Dhiyo yonah prachodayat.*[12]

Sai Baba has often explained the significance of the Gayatri mantra:

> *This is a universal prayer enshrined in the Vedas, the most ancient human scriptures. The Gayatri has three parts— praise, meditation, and prayer. First, the Divine is praised; then it is meditated upon in reverence, and finally, an appeal is made to the Divine to awaken and strengthen the intellect, the [truth-] discriminating faculty of*

12 The prayer translates as: "O Glorious Light illuminating the three worlds: the gross (physical), the subtle (mental), and the causal (spiritual); we meditate upon That, the vivifying power, love, radiant illumination, and divine grace of the universal intelligence. We pray for divine light to illumine all our minds."

> *man. . . . Never give up the Gayatri; you may give up or ignore any other mantra, but you should recite the Gayatri at least a few times a day. It will protect you from harm wherever you are—traveling, working, or at home.*
>
> —Sri Sathya Sai Baba[13]

As the evening progressed, more and more people came by, as soon as they heard what had happened. By midnight, stunt teams from both Universal Studios and Knott's Berry Farm had made their appearance, and then the actors from the Murder Mystery Dinner Theater came by, after their evening performance. The waiting room was full. Everyone had "Jay stories" to tell, and we all shed tears between the stories.

Ron and I were amazed by Jay's impact on these people. We'd had no idea. Everyone loved Jay, because he loved everyone and had the capacity to make them feel that he was their best friend. He loved to make people laugh, and he was good at it.

---

13 SSS 13:34, June 20, 1977.

We kept trying to piece together details about what had happened earlier that day. Jay had been performing in a mock gun shootout in the 2:30 p.m. "Calico Square" stunt show. He had been up on the water tower, equivalent to at least a second- or third-story balcony, about twenty-five feet above the ground. He played the part of being shot and falling dramatically from the water tower. A foam safety/landing pad was always strategically located, out of sight of the audience. Jay had practiced this type of fall time and again, even several times that very day. He was obsessive about safety and training. But whatever happened, the way he hit the pad, he bounced off and hit his head very hard on the pavement.

Only one person had witnessed the fall, a "spotter" on the stunt team. Jay had hit the mat but the mat had not sustained him. He had bounced off, hit his head on the concrete, and entered a coma immediately.

In the newspaper articles that appeared in the *Los Angeles Times* and the *Orange County Register* the next day, the spokesperson for Knott's was quoted as saying it was the first serious injury to a Knott's Berry Farm performer in the "50-year-plus history of stunt shows at the farm."[14] The fall in

---

14 Hickox, Katie. "Stuntman hurt in fall at Knott's," *The Orange County Register*, Mon. Aug. 22, 1994, Metro p. 1.

the performance was considered "routine," and Jay, being an "eight-year veteran of stunt shows," had performed this particular fall "hundreds of times."[15]

Sometime after midnight we were able to go into the intensive care unit and see Jay. He had been placed temporarily in the hallway until they had a bed for him in the ICU. Several members of the stunt team were also allowed to go in and talk to him if they wished to. I found out later that the nurse didn't believe Jay would live, so he let anyone who wanted to see Jay come in for a few minutes.

When I finally got to see Jay, my heart sank. He looked so pitiful, with tubes everywhere and his head completely bandaged. He was "posturing"—making movements that look like stretching, but we found out this was not a good sign. Posturing is involuntary motion caused by severe brain damage, when part of a muscle group is incapacitated. Also, pain can cause posturing. The amount and type of posturing helps determine the extent of the brain injury and to rate a person's coma level.[16]

---

15 Hall, Len. "Stuntman Hurt by Fall in Knott's Mock Gunfight," *The Los Angeles Times*, Mon. Aug. 22, 1994, pp. B1, B12.
16 The medical profession uses various scales to classify the level of coma, such as the Glasgow Coma Scale, the Rancho Los Amigos Scale, and others.

I talked to Jay, telling him he was going to be all right, but when I went back into the waiting room, I broke down and cried. The nurse told me it didn't look good, that Jay was in critical condition.

Finally, we learned that during surgery, the neurosurgeon had to remove a part of Jay's skull, in his right forehead area, in order to relieve pressure inside the cranium and help prevent further damage to the brain, as Jay's brain had swelled.

On Monday, the neurosurgeon told us that things were looking good. Jay was stable though still on a ventilator. The doctor felt Jay had a chance to come out of the coma. He told us that the injury had been on the right side of the head, which meant Jay would be able to talk, but not walk. But then he said that Jay might be taught to walk again, with therapy.

We felt good about this hopeful news, and that our prayers had been answered. But then, on Thursday morning, as I was sitting next to Jay's bed, talking and singing to him, the nurse said, "He's so sick! Don't you just get mad at God for times like these?" I wondered what she was talking about, since the doctor had told us on Monday that Jay was doing well and had implied that his prospects were good.

Then a social worker came in and asked, in a determined but cautious voice, "Does Jay have any siblings?"

I answered, "Yes, he has a sister in Kansas, but we're not going to have her come out until Jay is better."

Then she looked at me without smiling and said, with a more insistent tone this time, "Call her and have her come now!"

I was in a state of shock. I said, "Do you mean Jay is worse?"

She shook her head in the affirmative.

"Do you mean he might die?"

Again, she shook her head in the affirmative.

I immediately ran out of the room to find Ron, but he was nowhere in sight. The waiting room was still filled with some of Jay's friends, but I didn't want to say anything until I had talked to Ron. A message on the door had informed us that we were to meet with the neurosurgeon on Friday morning, but I figured that if it were an emergency, or if Jay's situation were really that dire, they would surely communicate with us before Friday.

I ran outside to the next building, the oncology center, and kept repeating to myself, "Lord, have mercy upon my soul and grant me peace." Near the oncology building, I found a sweet little garden that had some benches to sit on, so I sat there and broke down and wept. I had no inkling, no grasp inside me of the idea that Jay's karma in this life might be over, or that everything was just the way it should be. No, it would be a while before I could begin to understand this important concept. It's one thing to think about being detached; it's another when the idea of losing one's son looks like it's about to happen. I am sure that losing a child is one of the hardest things that any parent could ever face.

A little boy who looked about eight years old came up and sat down beside me. Gazing up at me, he asked, "Are you sad?"

I said, "Yes, I'm very sad. Do you pray?" I asked the little fellow.

"Yes," he said, still looking at me with questioning eyes.

"Well, I have a son, Jay, and he's very sick. Would you pray for him?"

Looking down at the ground, he said so sweetly, "Yes, and I have a mother; her name is Carol. She has cancer; would you pray for her?"

I said, "Yes, of course!"

So there in that little garden sat a mother praying for her son and a son praying for his mother. God has a great deal of compassion—and a sense of humor, I thought.

When I went back into the main hospital, I found Ron, who had just returned from an errand, and told him the news. We called Jan and told her to get ready to come to California as quickly as possible. She made plane reservations for the weekend, and my brother and his wife, and their daughter, Julie, also from Kansas, planned to come out with Jan's family. Julie was Kathy's sister, and both girls were very close to Jay and Jan, having all been born within a few years of each other.

Thursday had been a very busy day, and so emotionally charged. The news traveled around fast about Jay's condition, and that evening found the lobby of the hospital filled again with a multitude of Jay's friends and employees from Knott's Berry Farm. Because of Jay's personality and the way he knew and communicated with people, they were all there that night. The stunt crews, the musicians, the CEO of Knott's, and even one of the street sweepers, were there. Jay had befriended everyone, no matter their position. These folks all wanted to talk with our family and tell their stories of Jay, and many more tears were shed all around.

Ron and I went into the intensive care unit about 9:00 that evening to pray with Jay, and just to be with him for a few minutes. We ran into Paula, his wife, at the door of the ICU.

She asked us, "Did you see those three American Indians in their native costumes?"

We didn't know what she was talking about.

Then she said, "They were just here to visit Jay. They scared his nurse, and she wanted to know if the family had sent them."

Well, we hadn't sent them! We knew nothing about this. We didn't think much about it at first, in part because we figured it might have had to do with one of Jay's friends, Scott, a Native American performer at Knott's, who had worked with Jay at the Indian Village inside the theme park. Scott and eight of Jay's fellow stuntmen had performed a sweat lodge ceremony for Jay during that week, and we surmised that the visit from the Native Americans could have been a continuation of the sweat lodge.

A sweat lodge is a Native American spiritual ritual. Heated stones are placed in a pit in the middle of a teepee-like structure; water is poured over the stones, and the participants take off their clothes, sit in a circle, and sweat and pray and chant all night. The inspiration behind their sweat lodge that week was to give to Jay a part of themselves, to make him whole again.

We asked Scott later if the mysterious Native Americans who had visited Jay were a continuing aspect of the sweat lodge, and Scott replied, "No." He knew nothing of them and had no clue where they had come from.

We never found out who those Native Americans were. Logically, we should have passed them or seen them in the hall, but we hadn't. People in the lobby should have seen them, as the Native Americans would have had to walk through the lobby to get on the elevator to the ICU, but apparently, no one saw them. Finally, since Ron and I both have Native American blood in our family lines, we wondered if these visitors might have been ancestors from the spirit world. Perhaps, in a way, they were responding to the sweat lodge and everyone's prayers. Only two people saw these mysterious visitors—Jay's nurse and his wife.

When you have malaria, you have

to take bitter quinine medicine, which is

the medicine needed to cure the ailment.

Likewise, when adversity confronts you, you

should treat it as a medicine, as something

for your own good. Gold has to be melted

and beaten to make a jewel. A diamond

is cut to make it more brilliant. Likewise,

troubles in life serve to refine a person. Love

enables you to welcome even hardships as

meant for your own good.

—Sri Sathya Sai Baba[17]

---

17 SSS 29:52-2, November 23, 1996.

CHAPTER 4

MORE DEVASTATING NEWS
. . . AND A MIRACLE

It is not enough merely to share joy with each other; it is more important to share sorrow with each other. True friendship is that which enables one to help others at all times and in all circumstances. . . . You must transcend dissension and live in harmony by raising your hearts to God.

—Sri Sathya Sai Baba[18]

18 *Summer Showers, 1973,* ch. 30, p. 326, 330.

On Friday morning, during our scheduled meeting with the neurosurgeon, we received more devastating news—that Jay had experienced a stroke and grand mal seizure on Wednesday night, and that he had bleeding in the brain. They said that only the ventilator was keeping him alive at this point, and the doctor informed us that Jay would expire at any time. He asked us to take off the ventilator to make the transition faster and easier, but we asked to have it kept on until the rest of the family arrived on the weekend, so they could say their goodbyes, and the medical team agreed to this decision. We would wait five days, until the following Tuesday.

Then, as soon as we could, we drove over to the Sathya Sai Book Center in Tustin and sent a telegram to Prasanthi Nilayam[19], India, informing Sai Baba about Jay. We did this even though we believed that Sai Baba, in his omniscience and omnipresence, certainly would already know about Jay. But it is a custom among some devotees to take such actions in a time of need, also as an expression of faith and a form of prayer.

This dire news had brought out our grief again in full force, and our hearts were pained to the breaking point. Each of us seemed to have a

---

19 Prasanthi Nilayam, meaning "Abode of Highest Peace," is the name of Sri Sathya Sai Baba's main ashram in Puttaparthi, Andhra Pradesh, India.

different way of dealing with the grief; for me, it was as if I couldn't cry enough tears. But God sends angels when they are most needed. When we opened the door from the conference room after meeting with the neurosurgeon, there stood our friends, the Athertons, Steve and Katie. Steve was a psychiatrist, and Katie, a psychologist. Selflessly, they had been inspired to take time out of their busy practice to come and spend the day with us. They had anticipated that the news we would be receiving that morning would not be good, and they came to give their support. These were Sai devotees, and that is when we realized how wonderful these devotees were. They were living the teachings of our master, selflessly giving the love and service that they were capable of, as they became aware of our need.

Jan and Bill arrived later that day, with the boys and the rest of the family from Kansas. Steve and Katie helped Jan get through her initial grief. It was a poignant day, filled with much love and compassion.

On Saturday, Dr. Michael Goldstein and his wife, Gloria, also Sai devotees, came and spent five hours with us. Gloria brought food for the family—another godsend, as we did not feel like leaving the hospital even to eat. Just before these friends arrived, I had gone into the ICU and talked to Jay from my heart, saying goodbye in my way, as best

I could. I told him how much I loved him, and that I was going to let him go back to his Source, as it appeared his karma was over for this lifetime.

But when I told Dr. Goldstein what I had done, he ordered me, in no uncertain terms, "Go back in there and tell him to stay!" He reminded us firmly that Swami can do anything, and that he could change this situation at any moment. Then he suggested that we send Baba another telegram. So we did; we called Western Union from the hospital and sent another telegram.

A MIRACULOUS TURNAROUND

On Sunday morning, the family met again at the hospital, and we decided to go across the street to a restaurant for Sunday morning brunch. Though we hoped and prayed for Jay to live—for a miracle—we were all somber at the thought of saying our last goodbyes to Jay and counting down the last two days before Tuesday, the agreed-upon day for "pulling the plug."

As we were getting ready to leave for brunch, two more devotees came by—Bob and Rita Daniele, who had just returned from a stay at Prasanthi Nilayam in India. In fact, they had flown into Los Angeles International Airport at about the same time as Jay's fall the week before.

Rita pulled from her purse a small, silver, heart-shaped box; in it was some snowy-white *vibhuti* that Swami had materialized for her prior to her leaving India. Baba had told her at the time, "Don't eat it; take it home with you, and I will tell you who to give it to later." After Rita and Bob returned to the U.S., on that Sunday morning, in Rita's meditation, Baba had instructed her to take it to Jay, so she and Bob had come to the hospital to find us.

Ron and I were ecstatic and grateful. What comforting news! Like a divine mother, Sai Baba had anticipated this need—even before Jay's fall took place—and had already made provisions for us. At that moment, a strong feeling of certainty came over me that Jay was not going to leave us—that his destiny was to stay on board here on earth, at least for a while.

We talked about how we might give Jay the *vibhuti*. Normally we would try to have him swallow some, or at least place some on his tongue. I knew we would have a tough time getting him to swallow any, as his mouth was taped shut to keep the ventilator tubing in place, tubes that led down his throat. Bob suggested, "Well, just put some *vibhuti* on his forehead and under his nose; that should work."

Ron and I very quickly went up to the fourth floor to the ICU. We decided to sing the Gayatri mantra nine times before placing the *vibhuti* on Jay. Up until this moment, Jay had looked very still and nonresponsive, his face very dull and lifeless. Suddenly, as we were putting the *vibhuti* on his forehead and upper lip and chanting the Gayatri, Jay began to move his head, and a flood of life force seemed to enter his face; his look changed dramatically, and we could feel the difference immediately.

I dipped my finger in the *vibhuti*, then leaned over Jay and dabbed a small amount onto his forehead and another dot on his upper lip. Then he yawned, as if waking up from a long nap, and broke open the tape sealing his mouth! The timing was more than perfect. Our hearts leaped at this, and I thought for a moment that he was going to "wake up" at that point and start talking to us. While his mouth was open in this yawn, I quickly placed some of Baba's very fine, pure white holy ash on his tongue.

I knew he was going to live! Praise the Lord! Ron and I both started crying, and we spontaneously began repeating, "Thank you, Baba! Thank you, Baba!" We were filled with overwhelming gratitude.

We had been blessed, and we knew it. We also began to realize that this drama could have been set up years and even lifetimes ago. When Baba made the *vibhuti* for Rita, the accident hadn't even happened yet, but Baba was obviously aware of its eventual happening, and he had prepared Rita for her part in the play. Not a moment too soon, not a moment too late, at the perfect time and in this beautiful way, he let us know of his omniscience and ever-present care, and that he is the great stage director of our lives.

Our family had continued across the street to the restaurant, and afterward, when we joined them, I stood up and announced, "All of you saw our friends, Bob and Rita Daniele, this morning, and they brought some sacred ash right from Sai Baba's hands to give to Jay." I explained that Baba had materialized it for Rita in India and had told her internally, in her meditation that morning, to bring it to Jay. I continued explaining what had happened and that we felt it meant Jay was not going to die.

"This is such wonderful news," I said. "Let us all thank God for this morning's very special blessings."

There were a few *Hallelujahs* and *Amens*, but some of my family had deep reservations about this information. They all knew how Ron and I loved Sai Baba, and they weren't surprised, but they didn't understand the phenomenon either. And Jay was still in critical condition—but whatever it took to make Jay better and make him live, they were grateful for.

Each day thereafter, Jay got better. The nurses in the ICU were wonderful. They all worked with us in administering the *vibhuti* to Jay; when they used the thermometer, they would put a little of the holy ash in his mouth each time. In the ICU, Jay had a private nurse, one-on-one, who took care of only him. One day, his nurse that day, Bruce, came out of the room, pumped his fist in the air, and said, "Yes! Yes! Yes!" Jay's own breathing had begun to override the ventilator, a major step in terms of the recovery process, and when they took off the ventilator, Jay had breathed successfully on his own.

Another day, Bruce, the nurse, looked at the picture of Sai Baba we had placed on the wall beside Jay's bed. He said to us, "I see you have *him* on your side. Can you tell me a little more about him? My sister has his picture in her bedroom, but she won't tell me anything."

So we began to tell Bruce about Sai Baba and about some of the experiences we had had over the years. We also gave him a packet of *vibhuti*. He was very happy with the gift.

Later, Jay went into surgery to have a stoma or G-tube put in, a feeding tube leading directly to the stomach. Bruce accompanied Jay to surgery that day. Dr. Michael Goldstein had brought a white handkerchief that had been used by Sai Baba, to give to Jay, so we placed it on Jay. Bruce made sure this handkerchief went along with Jay to surgery, but somehow the handkerchief didn't come back from the surgery.

After the surgery that day, Bruce came to hug us goodbye; when I hugged him, he reeked of the jasmine-sweet fragrance of Baba's *vibhuti*. When I told him this, Bruce just laughed and said, "I wonder why!" We all said we wondered why, but we knew inside that a divine presence had been in the surgery room that day.

The following Friday, Jay was taken off the critical list and placed on the stable list. This good news came with a twist, however, because with this change in status, he lost his quarters in the ICU. They needed his bed for another patient. We were quite unhappy about this, because Jay was still in a coma.

છ

CHAPTER 5

IN REHAB

The next day, Saturday, Jay was transferred to Long Beach Memorial Hospital, where he was scheduled to begin rehabilitation therapy, even while still in a coma. We began to realize that this was the game plan in the medical and insurance world. They knew that Jay's chances of coming out of the coma were slim, and that he would probably be placed in a nursing home eventually. So they put these patients through a rehab of sorts, following the guidelines of the insurance company. After a certain time limit, they declare that the patient will not get any better, and then they place the person in a nursing home.

All during the time in the ICU and also in the Long Beach hospital, Jay was connected up to so many machines. Sometimes I would be with him and while listening to the *beep, beep* and soft gasps of the various machines, I would just despair, wondering if this was what the rest of his life was going to be like, or if this were to be the way in which we'd have to say goodbye to him. Sometimes the machines would give off a continuous alarm noise, and I would think, *This is it* . . . , and brace myself, expecting the worst.

One day I noticed something was wrong with Jay—his head was swelling. They had him lying down, without propping up his head, and I could see that his head was swelling up from being in this position. The nurse called the doctor, who ordered a CT-scan. When an orderly came by to take Jay for the scan, he asked us what the doctors had said about him.

I answered ruefully, "They weren't very encouraging and didn't give us a lot of hope."

"I knew it! I knew it!" the orderly exclaimed indignantly. "Listen, Mother! Those doctors don't know what they are talking about. They don't know! I can tell you right now, God is not through with this young man. He's gonna come out of it, and when he does, you're gonna want to have a party."

He poked me in the chest with his index finger. "Go ahead—have a party, invite everybody—but remember, no alcohol, because this is a party to thank God."

I was taken aback by this unexpected comment, so positive and expressed so strongly. I felt as if God were speaking right through this young man to me, giving me reassurance, and I felt very grateful. And the CT-scan disclosed that Jay was all right—the swelling had in fact been caused by not propping up his head.

VISITORS FROM MANY FAITHS

During Jay's stay at Irvine Medical Center and after he was transferred to Long Beach Memorial Hospital, many people, from many different religious backgrounds, came and prayed for Jay. We didn't invite people specifically; they just came of their own accord. Some were friends, of course, and the Sai Baba organization includes people of all faiths, but we had visits from the Catholics, the Charismatics ("In the name of Jesus, be healed!"), and the Mormons, who placed oil on his head. Many Hindus came, and also some Zoroastrians, who chanted their prayers while dangling a handkerchief above his body, which they moved slowly from his head to his feet. The Native Americans at Knott's Berry Farm did a healing dance during a performance one day. Every day, someone was there, praying by Jay's side. We were thinking, well, the only ones we hadn't heard from were the Muslims. Shortly after that we received a card, "May Allah watch over you."

One day, one of the stuntmen came by and talked to Jay. He said, "Jay, I haven't prayed in years, but I'm praying now with all my heart and soul."

These gestures and visits were very heartwarming for all of us. We didn't know or care what religion any of these groups belonged to; we felt that prayer is a universal language, and we were thrilled to witness this demonstration of all the different pathways to God. How wonderful! We were seeing one of Sai Baba's main tenets in action:

> *Every religion is a lamp that illumines the path to truth; every religion traverses the region of righteousness. Let the different faiths exist, let them flourish; let the glory of God be sung in all the languages, in a variety of tunes. That should be the ideal. Respect the differences between the faiths and recognize them as valid, as far as they do not extinguish the flame of unity.*
>
> —Sri Sathya Sai Baba[20]

20 *Sanathana Sarathi*, Dec. 1981, p. 274.

A couple of weeks after Jay was transferred to Long Beach Memorial Hospital, a church service was held in Jay's honor at the little white church inside Knott's Berry Farm. We were very touched by this gesture from the park and Jay's coworkers. The church, a tiny building with a white steeple was in the most picturesque setting, next to a small lake. Even though this church was inside a theme park, actual services were held on Sundays. All the musicians from the Knott's entertainment venues got together and participated in this service for Jay, which had a lot of music and singing. The church was jam-packed, with people standing outside, including many of the park employees and Jay's co-workers. One of Jay's friends, the park's Elvis impersonator, opened the service with "The Lord's Prayer." Another song, "One Day at a Time, Sweet Jesus," particularly spoke to me. The pastor of the church was impressed with the sound of all the voices singing in the church and said he would welcome such a group singing in the church any time.

LONG TERM CARE

We were assigned a psychologist at the Long Beach hospital. He took us into a room and explained more about the injury. He told us that in rehab they could take Jay as far as he could go, and then he would reach a place where there would be no further improvement. We would then have to make other arrangements for Jay's placement. We were introduced to a social worker to help us with these plans.

For a while at the Long Beach hospital, Jay was given hyperbaric treatments to bring oxygen to the brain, as part of his rehab therapy. He was assigned a certain number of treatments, and Jay seemed to respond to these treatments. I was with the hyperbaric doctor one day when he was testing Jay for progress. He talked to Jay and said, "Lift up your thumb," and Jay did it.

The doctor told me, "That action alone qualifies Jay for continuing hyperbaric treatments."

But the rehab doctor denied continuing Jay's oxygen treatments. We were sorely disappointed with this decision, which we did not feel was justified. It seemed to us, instead, to be a case of catering to the insurance company rather than to the patient. It is unknown whether continued hyperbaric treatments would have helped Jay, but they didn't even give him a chance when they denied further treatments.

This decision seemed so cruel and arbitrary that I completely lost hope at that point. Maybe I also had a backlog of emotion and tension over all the events that needed releasing, but at this frustrating news, I hit the wall. I was so depressed the next day that I couldn't wait for Ron to leave the RV that morning to go to the hospital. Alone in the RV, I cried all day. I didn't even go to the hospital that day. Inside me, something had snapped. I was feeling as if there were no hope at all.

Then Ron came home and talked about how great Jay was doing, how much color was in his face, and how well he seemed to be responding. That was great news, except that it was one of Jay's last days of receiving hyperbaric treatments, which made me feel sadder than ever. I'll always wonder if a great window of opportunity was missed there. It wasn't until a year later that we found another doctor, an osteopath, who gave Jay hyperbaric treatments in an independent facility, and we decided to pay for the treatments ourselves and leave the insurance company out of it, since they weren't willing to pay for the treatments.

Through this osteopath, who was also a nutritionist, we were able to put Jay on some very helpful supplements that would help keep his body healthy and make life a little easier for Jay as well as for us. The osteopath educated us about various nutritional strategies, including giving Jay DHEA and pregnenolone—precursor "building blocks" of many of the body's hormones. Ron was already a fan of nutritional supplementation, so we readily adopted this doctor's suggestions.

Jay had developed a film over his eyes that we couldn't seem to get rid of. Previously we had consulted with several ophthalmologists; one of them had suggested we just sew Jay's eyes shut—which we were not about to do. The osteopath, however, suspected that the film was a result of lack of DHEA. We started Jay on DHEA, and it worked; the film went away. We have continued to use such nutritional strategies, under medical supervision, with Jay.

Jay remained in the Long Beach hospital for the next three months, well into the fall season. This was the same hospital where he had been born twenty-nine years earlier, and we wondered daily about Jay's future. We stayed in our RV at an ocean-front campground in Long Beach, near where the historic ocean liner, the *Queen Mary*, is docked. It was a quiet, healing place for us, being right by the ocean. I could take long walks down by the ocean, and along a boardwalk that went to a little shopping center. We'd walk along the beach there, and those walks were my salvation.

Jay's friends continued to drop by and visit him in the hospital, in great numbers. They expressed their grief and felt very concerned about his condition. They showed so much love for him. Our niece, Kathy, also stayed for a couple of months and would spend up to eight hours a day with

Jay; she would talk to him, sing to him, and read to him, and also to other patients.

During this time, I was overwhelmed with grief, although I did not let the depth of it show to others, even to family members. On one hand I was trying to surrender to God's will and also to be grateful for everything, but on the other hand, I couldn't make sense of why this had happened; I was still in shock over it. Somehow we got through each day, one day at a time, making decisions and keeping up with all the changes and the near-constant stream of visitors, well-wishers, and friends. Many, many people were praying for Jay and us at that time, and they showed us a great deal of support.

But inside, my world had collapsed; my heart was broken, and the tears seemed always just below the surface. As soon as I was alone, they would flow unceasingly. I kept praying, "Your will, not mine," hoping to reach some peace.

Before Jay's event took place, I had been invited to speak in October at a Sai organization regional weekend retreat at La Honda in the San Francisco Bay Area, and to talk to the parents of the region about Education in Human Values—which is essentially bringing out the true virtues of the human being through a foundation of truth, right action, peace, love, and nonviolence. But with Jay's situation, and this event coming just five weeks after his hospitalization, I didn't see how

I could fulfill this commitment. I asked our friend Katie Atherton if she could go in my place. She proposed that we attend for just one day of the retreat, and that she would meet with the parents, and I would speak to the main group. I eventually agreed with that plan.

I wasn't able to prepare a talk; all I could do was turn it over to God. We arrived just one hour before our scheduled time, and as soon as I got up to speak, I could feel something unusual happening. I shared what had happened to Jay, and read out the quote about egoism that I had come across a few days before Jay's incident. I could relate only the bottom line: that grieving is ego, and everything that happens, has to happen. And even in saying this, I couldn't force myself to be in any place emotionally that I wasn't.

The room was so silent, not a dry eye anywhere. Spontaneously, afterward, a long line of people formed, and all they wanted to do was give me hug. That was an experience in itself. In the evening, the musicians dedicated a musical program to Jay.

After about three months, Jay was transferred to a combination neuro-care and rehab hospital. This facility just happened to be in Tustin, only two blocks from the Sathya Sai Book Center. We felt this to be another sign of Sai Baba's invisible but steady influence, another sign of his presence with us.

RON'S MEDICAL INTUITION

Jay was still having many medical problems, including a siege of emesis, or vomiting. The medical team was contemplating a surgery to insert a J-tube directly into the intestine; they felt this would stop the vomiting. Ron questioned this strategy and asked, "Why don't you try to find out the cause for the emesis instead of taking a shortcut to the solution, which may or may not work?"

Ron has the gift or talent of being able to go into meditation and get answers that he needs at the moment. Baba has given instruction, to us and to others, privately, on how to contact him if we need a question answered: go to a quiet place and sit in a meditative state, then proceed to ask our question. After this, we continue sitting quietly or doing whatever we need to do, and wait for an answer to come to us after a few minutes. Ron continues to use this process whenever needed.

Before giving permission for this surgery, Ron went into his meditative state and asked Baba what to do in this situation. The answer he got was to get a list of all the medications Jay was taking, and the times they were administered, and to compare this with the times of the emesis. As a result, Ron discovered three medications that could be causing the vomiting, and that two of these three medications should have been discontinued a few weeks before. The doctors cooperated with us, and Ron signed papers taking legal responsibility for removing these medications from the list. The medications were discontinued, and Jay stopped vomiting.

Another example of Ron's intuition concerned the surgery to replace a portion of Jay's skull—the part that had been surgically removed—by implanting a metal plate. The doctors were against it, because of the risk of introducing an infection to the brain during the surgery, which could be sealed in under the plate. Also, they thought that the skin layer might have become sealed to the brain, and that this would be a problem to detach without causing further damage.

But we were very concerned about this area, because there was only a thin layer of skin covering the brain itself. We thought the brain was at risk for more injury at this large soft spot, and infection could also easily result from any break in the skin that might occur while Jay was being handled, bathed, dressed, and so on. Ron kept getting very strong inner guidance to have the plate put in. When the surgery took place on October 31, 1995, the skin lifted up very easily; it was not at all attached to the brain, and the surgery was successful.

Since then we have had countless instances of this process of Ron receiving accurate inner guidance in Jay's case. Over the years, Jay's doctors have grown to respect Ron's input. Ron's own physician even kiddingly calls him "Dr. Ron"—and he gives Ron's opinion a lot of respect.

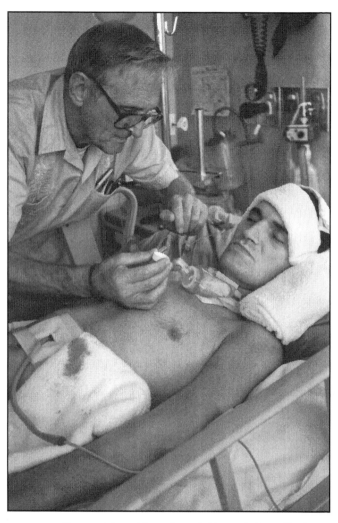

Ron and Jay at Long Beach Memorial Hospital (1994).

Ron is about to put some *lingam* water* in Jay's mouth.

(*See pp. 133, 136-139.)

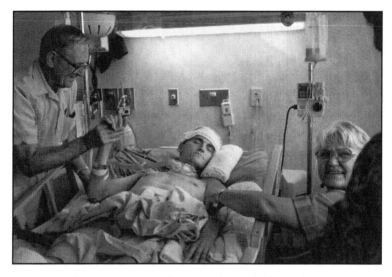

Ron, Jay, and Berniece keeping vigil with Jay at Long Beach Memorial Hospital. Jay's body had lost its ability to regulate temperature. He had a fever and we had to cool him with ice under his arms and a cold cloth on his forehead.

CHAPTER 6

DEALING WITH GRIEF

After the Thanksgiving and Christmas holidays, the rains came—and for me, more depression. I wondered where were we going with all this. By appearances, this was going to be a long term situation, and its implications were just beginning to dawn on us. Jay's care needs were intensive and ongoing. We were learning a lot very quickly, and doing all we could possibly do, but it was an overwhelming situation. All our former plans were now gone out the window, and we didn't even have a home, other than our RV. I wondered if I should resign my position as the National Education Coordinator for the USA Sri Sathya Sai Baba organization. I hadn't worked any more on the Teacher's Manual, and I felt at a complete standstill on that front.

My days were totally consumed by visiting Jay and visiting with family and friends as they continued to drop by the facility, and we had to continue monitoring Jay's care; we were very busy doing so and communicating with the employees of the facility.

Everyone has a different way of handling grief, and people do the best they can under the circumstances, but a life-change of this magnitude can stress the family bonds to the max. The change in Jay's life proved to be too much for Jay's wife, Paula; within three months she signed over all of Jay's affairs to us, and a divorce was granted the following year. Ron eventually became Jay's court-appointed conservator. We have seen this happen many times with the coma patients who have come and gone over the years in the facility where Jay lives—the family often breaks apart under the strain. Ron and I were fortunate in one way; being retired, we had the option of choosing to spend a lot of time with Jay. For younger families with children and those still active in the work force, the situation can be even more complex and demanding. We don't feel it is our place to judge people for their reactions and decisions; surely all those involved cope as best they can under such unexpected and almost unimaginable circumstances.

The people who knew Jay had a wide range of reactions. Although most of Jay's friends and co-workers came to see him, one of his closest friends on the stunt team could never bring himself to visit Jay.

Ron seemed to be able to maintain during the day; he immersed himself in caring for Jay, throwing himself into the challenges of this new situation, learning everything possible about the medical scenario and Jay's day-to-day condition. This occupied his mind. But it was in the middle of the night that his emotions would surface, and he would wake up with deep sobs in the wee hours of the morning.

Although some people would be angry at God for such an event, neither one of us reacted with this type of anger. Ron had always had reservations about the dangers of Jay's profession, but once this event took place, he accepted that there was little to be done except go forward as best as we could. Through our spiritual background, we both had an understanding of karma and reincarnation, and we could appreciate the fact that this was undoubtedly a karmic situation that we as a family were bound to experience.

This perspective helped Ron, especially. He felt that whatever happened, had to happen, according to a karmic agreement or to satisfy a karmic obligation, and the timeline or how it would resolve was not up to us to predict. He moved directly into the role of caring for Jay, and being legally responsible for Jay as his conservator.

Understanding Jay's needs required, on both our parts, not only a lot of ongoing observation but also the full extent of logical reasoning and deductive abilities, combined with intuition. It was a situation that demanded our full presence whenever we were with Jay, since Jay cannot speak for himself and has so many critical bodily needs. We learned mainly through ongoing experiences, over time, about his needs and how to care for him.

"THIS IS YOUR ROLE TO PLAY"

I was still getting through the days somehow, but my grief was acute, and it didn't seem to be letting up at all. In fact, it seemed to get worse as time went by. Then one evening a young man and friend of the family from Iowa, Michael Walsh, called and said to me, "Berniece, I think you should go to India and see Baba." Deep down, I had been thinking the same thing, but I didn't see how I could possibly justify leaving Ron and Jay at that time.

I stayed late with Jay one evening; Ron had gone home earlier. It was raining, and I just didn't feel like going home yet. Some years back, in 1986, Baba had called me to India through some song lyrics by Oleta Adams: "I Don't Care How You Get Here, Just Get Here If You Can." I frequently get spiritual messages through songs that happen to come on the radio, and nearly every trip I had taken to India until then, had some kind of theme song associated with it. That night, when I left Jay's room and went to my car, I turned the key, and of all things, I heard this same tune playing on the radio: "I Don't Care How You Get Here, Just Get Here If You Can"!

I broke down in tears, feeling it could be a sign that I should travel to India after all, despite my misgivings about leaving Jay and Ron. I cried all the way home, and then, as if underscoring this message, the song, "A Bridge Over Troubled Water," by Paul Simon, came on. This song spoke right to my heart, both hitting my feelings on the head and as a message from Baba. Two songs in a row had to be more than a coincidence. I knew then that I was definitely being called by Baba to come to India.

The next day, Michael called again and said, "Buy your ticket; I'm coming, and I'm going with you to India." I called the travel agent and was able to get a very good deal, traveling on the very dates that I wanted. I was suffering with mixed emotions, feeling a little bad and a little sad leaving Ron with Jay, but I knew I had to go. Besides, when the details fall into place so easily, it is another sign of the timing being right. I knew that if I weren't meant to go, the roadblocks would appear right and left, and it would be virtually impossible to get a ticket.

Less than two weeks later, Michael and I were on a plane to India. On that trip, we stayed at the ashram for only about ten days. Three days before we left the ashram, I was fortunate to be called by Sai Baba for an interview. In this interview, Baba answered all my questions and concerns. He said to the other people in the interview room, "She cries all the time. She cries in the car. She cries at home, in the house. She cries a lot." It was so true; I didn't talk about it with anyone and didn't even want Ron to know that I had been crying, feeling that he had enough to work through on his own without worrying about my grief. I would cry in the car or go into the bedroom; I would cry whenever I was alone, and I did cry a lot.

Baba talked about my work as National Education Coordinator. When I started to say that I planned to go around the country leading teacher trainings, wondering inside if I should give up this plan, he stopped me right there and said, "Yes! You do that! Start doing!"

He then told us that all this world or life is a big drama, and that we are all actors on this stage; we each have a role to play. He said to me, "This is your role to play!" Then he sat back in his chair and exclaimed, "And I'm the director!"

I told him that I was having a tough time getting the teacher's manual finished because of needing to be with my brain-injured son.

He said to me, "Why are you so attached to this son? How many sons have you had? Do you remember any of them?"

I realized that he was referring to past lives, and of course I didn't remember any of them, or any of the children I might have had in those lives.

He then told me to get the teacher's manual finished, and I answered, "I'm trying."

He commanded, firmly, "Don't try, DO!"

He placed his index finger on the middle of my forehead and said, "I'm blessing you; I'm directing you. Have confidence!" He told me not to worry, that things would get better very soon. He talked about Ron and Jay, and said, "Don't worry; I'm taking care of everything."

Then he continued, "Nothing bad ever happens! You see, it's like this: tonight you eat fruit and think it's good; tomorrow, it's waste, and you think it's bad. It's all the same!" He was referring to *karma* (our actions and their results) being played out, and that just because we cannot see the whole picture, we judge things as "bad—things that in the larger scheme of events, the divine drama as directed by the divine director—are not "bad" at all. We must learn to accept all of life's ups and downs in a spirit of equanimity, trust, and faith. Easier said than done!

Before going to darshan that day, I had been reading Phyllis Krystal's book, *Taming Our Monkey*

Mind.[21] I had read this book on the airplane, so that day I just randomly opened the book, and a penny fell out on my chest. I thought this was rather strange, as I never take any money change with me to India, and I had just read the book. I wondered, where did this penny come from?

Then I read the page, which was about "Surrender, Trust, and Accept." The author used this phrase as a kind of faith mantra, meaning, "*Surrender* to the High Self, *trust* It to bring about whatever It knows is needed, and *accept* whatever that may be."[22] This was a lesson I was beginning to learn on this trip. Then I picked up the penny and read the inscription, "In God We Trust"—an instant and concrete emphasis on the lesson being given to me. Then, that very day, Baba called me for the interview.

During that interview in January 1995, Swami had said, "Things will get better very soon; you will see." The "very soon" turned out to be a series of gradual changes over the next nine months. First, our living conditions were rather difficult, as we were still "making do" out of our motor home, which was camped in an RV park in Tustin, about two miles from Jay. A motor home is fun to live in when you are traveling to different places, but as

---

21 Krystal, Phyllis. *Taming Our Monkey Mind: Insight, Detachment, Identity* (York Beach, Maine: Samuel Weiser, Inc., 1994).
22 *Ibid.* p. 34.

a permanent home, it is not so much fun. We had already lived in the motor home for fifteen months.

Then, in the fall of 1995, through a Sai devotee in Tustin, we learned of a double-wide mobile home for sale at a reasonable price in a seniors-only mobile home park in Tustin. The park had a beautiful garden-like setting, with flowers and orange trees. We bought the place and moved in. Now we had two bedrooms, two bathrooms, and, in comparison to our RV, plenty of room. How wonderful. It was easy moving from the motor home into the mobile-home house, but moving to such a small place from our former big house would have been traumatic for me. Everything is relative. God works in strange and wonderful ways, doesn't he, because now I was very grateful to have this new living space.

Over these months, as I contemplated Baba's "very soon" message, I realized that things were in fact getting better. Not only had our living situation improved but Jay was stable; they had removed his "trache" (tracheostomy) tube. He was responding well to therapy. He was getting regular acupuncture treatments, along with range-of-motion exercises and massage to keep his muscles from atrophying.

Not only that, but by November 1995, a preview copy of the new and greatly expanded *Sai Spiritual Education Teacher's Manual* was ready to take to

India, with our hopes of receiving Sai Baba's approval to proceed with getting it printed. Baba had blessed and helped with this too, "sending" the perfect people to help complete this major publication.

A world conference of the international Sai organization was scheduled to take place in Prasanthi Nilayam that November, in conjunction with Sai Baba's 70th birthday, in the days surrounding November 23. I attended the conference, and while we were there, Sai Baba blessed the teacher's manual for publication, saying "Very important book," which was wonderful to hear. And although I did not get called for an interview during that trip, I met a person who would become a significant link in Jay's story.

I had been given permission with three other ladies to stay in an apartment in the ashram that belonged to some personal friends, the Kaplowitzes. They had lived inside the ashram while their daughters were attending Sai Baba's school. One of the ladies also staying in this apartment was Jackie, a medical doctor from Stanford University; she was volunteering as a doctor during the 70th birthday festival and world conference. Dr. Jackie and I became fast friends; I would spend time with her again the next time I traveled to India, and she would introduce me later to Debbie, who was to become a key player in the divine drama of events involving Jay.

THE STREET-LIGHT DRAMA

At some point after Jay moved to the long-term rehab facility, we began noticing a very odd phenomenon. Often, just as we were driving to or from our nightly visit to Jay, we would pass a street light and it would flicker and go out. Sometimes this happened on our way to the facility, but most frequently it happened right after we left the place. Pretty soon we began to wonder if this had something to do with Jay, if he were somehow influencing the street lights to go out. This also happened other places around town; pretty soon, whenever it happened, we started saying, "Oh, that must be Jay!" We had no idea what was causing this, but it happened so often around us that we started associating it with Jay.

"WHY WORRY ABOUT JAY?!"

Over the next year, after the *Sai Spiritual Education Teacher's Manual* got published, I began giving SSE teacher trainings and seminars around the country. There are ten regions in the U.S. Sai organization, and trainings needed to be held in each region. Sai Baba had given explicit instructions that I was to do this work, and by this time we had established more regular routines for Jay's care, and I could leave Ron and Jay for these mostly brief travels.

In February 1997, I traveled again to India with my sister, Vera, and a few others for a quick, twelve-day trip. Like the one in January 1995, this trip got set in motion by our family friend from Iowa, Michael Walsh, who once again called me up out of the blue on a January morning, saying, "Don't you think it's about time to go see Swami?"

Ron, at this time, still did not wish to leave Jay long enough go to India. So, off we went to India, and while at the ashram that February, I met up again with Jackie, the doctor from Stanford. It was so good seeing her, as I hadn't been in touch with her since we had met, fifteen months earlier, in November 1995. This time, about halfway into our eight-day stay at the ashram, I became very ill and had to spend a day in bed with a high fever and stomach upset, and Jackie came and took good care of me. It was like having my own private physician, one who even made house calls.

During that week, she mentioned to me a friend of hers, saying, "Berniece, you have to come to San Francisco and meet Debbie. We are doing a lot of children's art work, and I think you will like what we are doing; you might want to use some of the ideas for the children's program."

This sounded like a good idea, so I told her I would certainly make plans to come, but I would have to look for a convenient time, as I was very busy with teacher trainings and workshops around the country.

The day before we were to leave, Sai Baba called our small group and a few others into the interview room. This was a wonderful interview. He spoke to us about our personal problems, our health problems, and gave us advice on how to make our lives better. He materialized *vibhuti* for us and gave us packets of *vibhuti* to take home with us.

I asked him about Jay. "Swami, does he have a mind?"

Swami answered, "Oh, yes. Mind is everything; mind is everywhere. Mind is all he has—he has no body . . . body is not good."

Michael jumped into the conversation, asking, "Jay is going to be all right, isn't he, Swami?"

Swami answered in a chastening tone, his voice rising with each syllable, "*Jay! Jay!! Jay!!!*[23] *Why* do you worry about *Jay?!*"

When Baba said this, I knew then that it was time to stop asking questions about Jay. Baba had already let me know in 1995 that he was taking care of Jay. I also knew that Jay was aware of the

---

23 Every action or gesture, every word, of the avatar has a deep meaning, and often a meaning with several layers. In Southern India, the exclamation, *Jai!*—pronounced identical to the English name, *Jay*—means "Victory!" and is often repeated several times in songs of praise to the Lord, as in *Jai! Jai! Jai!*

people around him and the conversations we had. And yes, I knew that Jay had a very active mind. Later that year, I would meet Debbie, who would be able to communicate with this mind that Baba had said was everything and everywhere. For it would be through Debbie that we would start to receive "letters" from "J."

༄

The world is a stage. We are all actors in the world drama. But all our actions are motivated by God, who controls our immortal souls and perishable bodies. And we must play the game without displaying any sort of weakness or timidity. . . . Spirituality and equanimity go together.

—Sri Sathya Sai Baba[24]

---

24 *Summer Showers in Brindavan 1979*, ch. 5, p. 38.

CHAPTER 7

"J"

> *The mind can run faster than light. . . .*
>
> *Thought waves emanating from the mind*
>
> *have also got properties of radio waves.*
>
> *There is no end to the waves arising from the*
>
> *ocean of the mind. The power of thought is*
>
> *immense. Thoughts outlast the human body.*
>
> *Thought waves radiate very much like heat*
>
> *waves, radio waves, and light waves.*
>
> —Sri Sathya Sai Baba[25]

The rest of the year 1997 proved to be very busy for me. I traveled in the late spring to St. Petersburg

---

25 SSS 21:25, May 23, 1993.

and Moscow, Russia, giving a workshop to public school teachers in St. Petersburg on Education in Human Values and a workshop on Sai Spiritual Education to Russian Sai devotees in Moscow. I also kept up the teacher trainings in the U.S. and a speaking schedule at retreats and conferences for the Sai organization. I seemed to be having trouble getting to San Francisco to see Dr. Jackie and to meet her friend Debbie. It was looking as if a trip to San Francisco were not going to happen that year.

But then Jackie called me the last week in September. She reminded me that I had not kept my promise. "Berniece, when are you coming to San Francisco to meet Debbie?"

I had an immediate, small window of time between trips and replied, "Well, as a matter of fact, I have this next weekend off. Can I come that soon?"

She said, "Yes, of course. I'll call Debbie, and we'll make arrangements for your visit."

I met Debbie and stayed with her family that Thursday evening. The San Francisco Sai Center met in their apartment, so we attended the meeting that evening. Then, on Friday, with Debbie's family and Dr. Jackie, we traveled to the city of Sonoma, where the family had a beautiful home out in the wine country. I was anxious to see the artwork the girls were doing, and to relax and have a good weekend—for once without having to speak or conduct a teacher training. I was "on vacation," in the company of good people, the countryside was beautiful, and the weather was gorgeous. I felt connected with Debbie right away, and with Jackie—the three of us had lots of laughs and a good time visiting.

During dinner on Friday evening, Debbie's husband began to tell me about Debbie's talents. He explained that she could communicate with people on the "other side," and that after dinner she was going to meet with a medical student from Stanford University who wanted to talk with her about his spiritual guides—wanting his spirit guides to meet with her spirit guides from the other side.

I began then to wonder if I had come to the wrong place. Just what was going on? Was this some kind of hocus-pocus? Debbie was so sweet and unassuming in her conversation that I felt very comfortable with her, and she didn't seem to me like a medium. Ron and I had dabbled in the "medium" track when we had attended some metaphysical churches in Orange County, but now, this was with Sai devotees, and I had a few doubts. My mind is always capable of giving me a sad time in things I have no understanding about, and this was one of them.

But it was an intriguing subject, and after our conversation at the dinner table, I asked Debbie,

"Do you think you could communicate with Jay?" She answered so sweetly and innocently, "Oh, I don't know; we can try. Tonight when I go to do the work with this young man, I'll see if we can find Jay."

Their home was a large, rambling, three-story country house. We all went to a quiet room on the first floor, where we were going to see about talking with "the dead"—people in spirit form. Debbie said that first we had to clear the air of any negative thoughts. She didn't want to be bombarded with any negative entities, which I guess sometimes try to take advantage of such situations and play a little havoc. So we all became very quiet, chanted some *Oms*, and I started feeling a very cool breeze on my face.

I thought at the time, "There must be a fan running or a window open somewhere," so I opened my eyes to see where this cool breeze was coming from. To my surprise, there was nothing in the room to cause this breeze on my face. I had heard of people feeling a cool breeze when someone in "spirit form" comes in close. So I thought, "Well, I guess we're being visited by some folks from the other side." I tried not to worry about it, to get into the moment and be broadminded in my thinking.

I felt that these were good, sincere people, and I wondered if maybe there were a reason, beyond the surface, for my having come to Northern California. Maybe I was, at long last, really going to be able to communicate with Jay, and I became a little anxious—hoping this was true.

Then Debbie said, "Jay is here, and he has something to tell you." Despite our preparations and my hopes, this announcement took me by surprise. I was in a state of shock, and I hoped with all my heart that this wasn't just someone's imagination. I knew already that Jay could hear us when we spoke to him in his physical presence, because he could answer us with a "yes" or "no" by blinking his eyes, but he wasn't able really to converse with us.

I had felt his immense frustration at times, sensing clearly that he wanted to say something. This palpable frustration had been much worse in the beginning when he opened his eyes and couldn't speak; over time I felt he had accepted his situation and very gradually come to terms with it, of sorts.

Sai Baba had told me earlier that year in February that Jay had a mind—that *mind was everything, mind was everywhere, mind was all he had*, and that the body wasn't good. So could this really be Jay communicating with me—Jay's mind, or Jay as a conscious entity in spirit, able to move around out-of-body and come to Debbie and her vibration? I wondered.

Through Debbie, Jay began to mention things that were meaningful to me—things that Debbie could not have known. But I had no tape recorder, no one was taking notes, and I remembered very little of what he told me. He did talk a little about his "accident" and said he was going to write us a letter. This set my mind to bouncing around again, and I wondered, "Now how is he going to write us a letter?" It didn't make sense to me.

I remember very little of how the session ended, as I was still in a state of shock or disbelief. I asked Debbie how Jay was going to write us a letter. She said in her matter of fact way, "I don't know. Just pay attention to any mail you get from anyone."

I thought at the time, "Well, that isn't something I can do very well." But I decided to remain open. I had no idea what Jay had meant by "writing a letter." The conversation lasted approximately fifteen to twenty minutes; then it was over.

All in all, I accepted the possibility that this could have been a communication from Jay, and I wanted to remain open-minded about it. I had no idea what to expect next.

But it was only a week later when I received a call from Debbie. She said to me, "Jay came to me this morning, and I have a letter for you. Do you want me to fax it to you?"

I was very anxious to read such a letter and said, "Yes, please do!" And so, on October 9, 1997, we received our first written communication from Jay through Debbie.

LETTER 1

Thursday, October 9, 1997, 8:50 a.m. – 10:39 a.m.
San Francisco, California

JAY: First of all, I want to thank you for your making yourself available as my "scribe" ("secretary" sounds demeaning). There are a number of things I want to tell the folks, and this is a workable station. It's hard to remain even-tempered when so many emotions swing back and forth (between me and my family and friends), but this is an opportunity to express myself fully, and by golly, I'm going to use it. I prefer just the initial "J" for my name. And I would prefer using pencil rather than pen to write with.

DEBBIE: Okay. What is the significance of "J" from "Jay," and why a pencil over a pen? Just curious.

J: I always appreciated symbolic meanings to things—like the underlying meaning behind the surface interpretation. That way, if someone didn't understand the deeper meaning of something, they still got the surface meaning (without feeling "dumb"). And for those who <u>did</u> get the deeper meanings of symbolic gestures, it would amuse, entertain, and spark their interests. Also it is a way of flushing out the ones who "get it" from the ones who are not ready yet. I always like to know who and what I'm dealing with.

So, "J" (instead of "Jay") is in the middle of the alphabet (plus it's quicker to write, this way). And that's where I am right now. I'm in the middle, because this is exactly where I'm supposed to be. It's where I've trained all my worldly life to be—make no mistake. I've worked very hard to get here, and from my perspective, here, it's a precarious place to attain—not many people are allowed to aspire to be in a limbo state like this. Only a few, a few.

Although it may not seem so from your end of things and the way my physical body "appears"— I'm a very busy person! So, don't spend any time feeling sorry for me, or even for yourselves; this is a much sought-after position and privilege, not to mention a lot of hard work. You think that because my physical body is fairly immobile that I'm trapped inside. Wrong. I'm as free as a bird, and yet I still maintain the physical form (which requires a lot of energy and constant monitoring for balancing the equilibrium inside) in order to connect with all of you who are in the body still.

Just as you think you are helping me (and you are, believe me!—your prayers, attention, and energy go a long way into keeping this bodily form functional), I am also close to you, helping you. We are together walking on the spiritual path. I know you know there are no accidents, no coincidences. And I know you know the symbolic significance of my career as a stuntman. Doing stunts was the ultimate high in creating the illusion of something happening—out of which the end result was truly not real, i.e., death by gunshots, etc. It was all training—life is the ultimate training exercise. And when we're ready for the test, we pass it according to the amount of effort and care we took in the practice sessions.

Why do you think I was so careful about safety—meticulous to every detail—about the pratfalls? Other stunt people around me would sometimes joke around, be goofy, and treat it lightly at times. Not me! That's why I was always harping at them to check their gear, their moves, their program, ahead of time. And still, to this day, I'm on their cases, nagging at them to take this seriously—not just for safety's sake (although that's a number one issue at all times), but also because life's training exercises, each and every one of them, are so important. They are not to be taken lightly, by any means.

My injury was no accident—stop calling it an "accident." When you refer to it as an "accident," the implication is that it was unplanned, unfair, and that my life was all for nothing. Wrong again! (Am I being too critical or hard on you? Sorry if it sounds like that; you know that I care very deeply for you all.) I simply graduated <u>right on time</u>.

You cannot imagine how complicated it is to keep this body going while also working in other places! Partly, the physical form is still operational due to God's grace—your well-earned bank account of merit that you've been building up all these years. Just don't overdraw the account! (smile)

The other reason for keeping the physical body going is that it is acting as a catalyst for those around it to progress further on their own paths. I guess you could say it's all God's grace, come to think of it. (smiling) How did we get off on this tangent?!?

Okay, so I'm in the so-called middle of things. You cannot imagine how many people you have touched and influenced all over the world since my transitional experience—("T.E." or "experience," you can call it—not "accident")—not just those who have come to see me as the body, but many more who have been touched by the story.

Mom, you have to write your story in this vein—no pun intended. (smiling) You know, <u>before</u> my experience, you totally dedicated yourself to Swami, to the organization (don't let it get to you), and to teaching. And, yes, your intention came from the heart via the mind, but the mind always interfered with the basic, original intention (clouding it with even a little of the old ego), so that there was always a little cloudiness in the final presentation. You know, Mom—that "want of control" that we all know so well and have such a time of battling with inside? From the day of my experience, you completely by-passed the mind and communicated <u>totally</u> from the heart. In other words, you told your mind to "take a hike!" It wasn't useful in dealing with emotional shock.

I'll bet you wonder if Baba was here to help me when that happened! It was really strange, but funny too. I always like a good joke and lots of laughs! When I saw my body all twisted after the fall, I was confused at first. How could I be looking at myself and not feeling any pain? At first I thought it was one of the other guys, in fact, and was horrified to see what had happened! Always did feel responsible for everyone else. Anyway, all at once, I saw Swami next to me—standing right next to me, looking down at the body. Then I <u>knew</u> I was dead. So I said to Swami, "Does this mean I'm dead?"

And he said to me, so sweetly and slowly, "No, not dead, just sleeping."

I watched the paramedics come and take the body away. Swami was still next to me. He put his arm and hand around my shoulder and said, "Good boy! Be happy. Now, get back to work."

I wasn't sure what he meant (so what else is new?), but I followed everyone around—trying to boost morale. That went on for some time, I can tell you. And then I found myself involved in helping others adjust to the loss of the physical body—mainly young children and teenagers who had suddenly and unexpectedly lost their bodies. Well, not lost, but literally spring-boarded out of their bodies. Just like diving off of a building in free fall—only this is literally "jumping out" of the body suddenly. The younger children are harder to help, because they've just barely become used to operating within the dense constraints of the body. The teenagers adjust much more readily—you know, anything for a thrill. I am also counseling others, working with addicts of one kind or another, and checking in with you guys in my so-called "spare time."

Mom and Dad, I can't thank you enough for all the great things you've done for me and continue to do!! I mean it—every gesture, all your prayers, and everyone's good "vibes" help me tremendously.

Dad, I'm going to speak a little to you now. I know deep down inside you, you feel like somehow this could have been prevented, "If only . . . ." You really <u>have</u> to know that this is what I wanted, what I planned for, worked hard for. Think of the alternative—I could/would <u>still</u> be doing my job, in my body, with very limited contact or influence on those I'm around and those I love. Limited—it would be a delay, even a waste, to restrict myself. Would you keep your son from graduating out of high school just because your contact with him would alter due to his going to a university (get it?) "far" from home? Of course, not!

Also ask yourself, would you keep your son "home" when he was offered a plum assignment in God's educational program?!? What would you say to Swami—"No, I think Jay should stay here, pedaling his bike in a stationary position, until I'm 'gone'"? You have <u>to trust</u> me, Dad. I will never leave you behind. Never.

That goes for you, too, Mom. I haven't "gone" any-where—and I'm working twice as hard as I used to. I'm still <u>here</u> (with or without a physical body). Baba is still here. Yes, you can have *darshan* here, too, but the crowds are ten times (or more) the size <u>here</u> than <u>there</u>! But the nice thing is that if you want to speak to Swami, or vice-versa, he will <u>instantly</u> appear—according to karma, divine will, etc. Same thing <u>there</u> where you are, but you just don't see him. Get the doubts out of the way! Your doubts and wavering are the heavy curtains that cloud your inner vision.

I have to stop here. D is getting tired. To Kim—I do <u>not</u> have a girlfriend here—you know that! (This is private.) (smiling) And yes, I take the dog every-where with me—still a great mutt! We are good company for each other.

As to the pencil—I always had more preference for a pencil as a "safety net" (get it?), in case I made a mistake "by accident." Love you all deeply from my heart!

—Your Loving Jay

To say the least, we were blown away by this communication from Jay. We were in awe to think that this was even possible, and it certainly sounded like Jay to us, but I still had many doubts about the whole thing. On the other hand, who else could talk with such authority, accuracy, and even professionalism about what had happened to him and about the stunt work he had been involved in?

The depth at which he addressed us, we found amazing. This letter was not just chit-chat and "how's it goin', folks?" No. Instead, Jay—or "J," as he asked to be called in the letter—got straight to the heart of things—"shooting from the hip"— giving us much to ponder on a very personal level, and opening our eyes and minds on so many fronts. He was talking to us about our innermost— even subconscious—thoughts and feelings. It was as if, just as he said, he was going to use this opportunity to express the maximum possible, get the most mileage out of every word, and at the same time plant seeds in our thinking that could help us heal and make progress in various ways.

In the first few lines, he used the phrase, referring to Debbie, ". . . this is a workable station." One of the dictionary meanings of *station* is "the place or equipment for sending out or receiving programs or messages by radio or television." We also think of a *station* as a "channel"—as in tuning a piece of equipment, such as a television or radio, to a certain broadcasting channel or frequency. This sounded a lot like how Debbie and Jay were connecting. These words sounded "so Jay," and I could imagine him saying something just like that.

It was of course comforting—and humorous— to picture Sai Baba coming to him after his fall and telling him, "Now get to work," and to think that Jay was so busy and active, despite his physical appearance, even if we had a hard time understanding how this was so. Naturally we had times of wondering whether all our efforts were doing any good or having any effect, and it was tempting to feel discouraged at times, so it was also encouraging to hear how all the prayers, attention, and involvement had been significant and helpful.

Right off the bat he acknowledged his frustration at not being able to speak, which I had picked up on many times, and the varied emotions that we all experienced together. And he talked about how much effort went into monitoring and balancing his body equilibrium; our efforts were (and are) constant on this front, and he seemed to imply that he is very actively involved in this monitoring and balancing process also, and that it's hard work for him, too.

For one thing, his body does not currently have the capability of regulating its own temperature, so we have to constantly watch for chilling and overheating, and adjust his amount of covering to keep his temperature stable. Also, any build up of fluid and mucus has to be suctioned out of his breathing passages, as he cannot always cough or clear his own passages.

There are times when he is placed back into his bed or in his wheelchair, when his clothes get bundled in a knot behind his back or under his seat, or his body is placed crooked in bed or in his chair, and it becomes uncomfortable for him. When this happens, he coughs and keeps coughing, moving his face and arms, and pulling his head backward until someone comes and fixes the problem.

He has gone into a seizure when he was so uncomfortable, and no one noticed, at a time when we weren't there to address the situation. This is one of the reasons we spend so much time with him, because it is impossible to monitor him one-on-one at all times.

All the fluids and nutrition going in and the wastes coming out also have to be closely monitored. In other words, many of the normal processes of how a human body keeps its inner balance are at least partially disrupted in Jay's case. Because his pituitary function was impaired, many of his other endocrine functions are affected. It was a big help when we discovered how to make use of DHEA and pregnenolone—precursors or building blocks of many hormones—thanks to the osteopath's recommendation. These have helped to supplement some of the endocrine function, but we have to request special lab work to monitor Jay's DHEA levels. Commercial laboratories that analyze the actual blood serum DHEA levels are rare, so we have to send the blood work out of state and keep checking up after the local labs so that they do not process the wrong DHEA tests.

These are just a few of the bodily conditions and needs that we check on continuously. Jay also communicates with us—by blinking and other gestures, such as coughing to get someone's attention, as mentioned above.

Jay also talked about following us around—and his co-workers—boosting morale and even "nagging" the stunt team to be serious about their work. He chided me about my doubts and emphasized that we were all walking together somehow on the spiritual path. He seemed to be saying that there was a definite spiritual purpose behind his being in this condition.

Jay sent a brief personal message in this letter to his friend, Kim—someone Debbie had no knowledge of at all. Kim was one of Jay's friends from Knott's Berry Farm, and she has continued to visit Jay over all these years.

Jay also mentioned the dog. We could only figure this was our family dog, Caleb, whom we all missed very much. Caleb had been a blond-haired friendly mutt that Jay and Jan had picked up outside the pound after our family came home from a trip to India in 1982. While we were in India, the stray dogs in the ashram had followed Jan around and lain at her feet. Back in California, just as Jay and Jan got to the pound, even before they went inside, they saw this dog. A veterinarian's wife was outside the pound; the dog had been abandoned in the middle of a freeway, thrown out of a car, and its leg was cut. It was only about four months old. The vet's wife didn't want to put the dog in the pound, so Jay and Jan took him on the spot, and we had him for eleven years.

Caleb got along with our three cats; in fact, he seemed to think he was a cat. He groomed the cats and liked to jump up high on things like they did. Although we kept him outdoors, he used to sneak into Jay's window and sleep with Jay. When we had to put Caleb down in 1993, it had broken our hearts. Looking back, that took place within a year of Jay's transitioning experience. So it sounded to us as if Caleb were still around Jay—or our family—in the other dimension where Jay operates.

This was not information we could take in all at once—far from it. So much was presented in this letter, which we read and re-read many times—and still re-read and get more out of, even years later.

∾

CHAPTER 8

DEBBIE'S VISIT TO JAY

After receiving Jay's first letter, we felt we had received some answers to what this drama was all about, but we still wavered in our thinking. Could this actually be Jay's experience? Was he really doing all this work on another plane? We tried to remain open-minded, and we felt some peace—and gratitude—for having received the information. It sure sounded like Jay.

One of the last performances we saw Jay in had been at Knott's Berry Farm. He was doing crowd control, performing as a "mime." He chose a small boy from the audience and had this kid pulling an imaginary gun from an imaginary holster—they had a stand-off without any words. The crowd loved it, and I thought at the time, "I believe Jay is communicating with the little kid with his mind," because this kid was doing the pantomime just like Jay, without any words. So maybe Jay had some already-developed gifts in this area of mental communication.

I remember saying to Ron, "You know, Jay is really talented; he's a good actor, but also he works with children very well." Jay had always had a special knack with the small children in the extended family, as well as those of our friends and the school children I worked with. In the SSE children's classes I taught in our home, one of the students was a little boy named Billy who had Down's syndrome. Jay loved Billy and would work with him. Billy never forgot Jay and even came to visit him after Jay entered the coma. Children always seemed drawn to Jay, but that was because Jay loved them, too.

As we were contemplating the contents of the first letter, we had no idea what would happen next, or if this kind of communication would continue. But only one week after receiving Jay's initial letter, we received a call from Debbie. She had been communicating with Jay, and Jay wanted her to come to Southern California, to visit him and see him in his body.

"Would you mind if Jackie and I flew down tomorrow and spent the day and the night, and we'll go home the next day, on Wednesday?"

Of course, we were delighted that they would take time out of their busy schedules to come and visit us. I told her, "Please do come—and let me know your flight number and time you will be arriving, and I will pick you up at the Los Angeles International Airport (LAX)."

Early on Tuesday morning, October 14, Dr. Jackie and Debbie arrived at the Los Angeles airport, and we drove together back to our home in Tustin, in Orange County, about forty-five minutes from LAX. We had a leisurely breakfast and a nice visit before going to see Jay at the neuro-care facility near Tustin, in the foothill area called Cowan Heights. This area was named after Walter and Elsie Cowan and once had been part of the Cowans' land holdings. Walter had been an oil magnate and land developer, and the Cowans were among the earliest American devotees of Sri Sathya Sai Baba; in 1971, Walter had been raised from the dead by Swami, and Elsie had donated the land and building, in Tustin, for the Sathya Sai Book Center of America.

It was a warm day, with what we call "Santa Ana winds" blowing, and as often happens at that time of year under those conditions, fires were beginning to erupt around Southern California. One fire was in the foothills surrounding Jay's facility. The facility was placed on emergency alert, which meant we could be evacuated at any time, day or night.

We decided not to be concerned about the fire conditions and to continue with our visit as planned. Debbie and Dr. Jackie met Jay and some of the nurses and CNAs, as well as some of the other patients. We spent a couple of hours visiting there before returning home for lunch. That afternoon Debbie went into the bedroom and received another letter from Jay. This letter was addressed mainly to Ron and the concerns he was feeling at that time.

LETTER 2

Tuesday, October 14, 1997, 4:23 pm – 5:44 pm
Tustin, California

D: Okay, Jay. We're ready to receive. It was really a wonderful experience coming down here to see you and your parents and to be able to have this experience. Thank you for inviting us here.

J: Thank <u>you</u> for listening and for following your heartfelt instincts so carefully! It's not easy to find someone to work with, set up meetings, and convince people that I'm really <u>all here</u>. It's truly amazing all the many things we take for granted when we're "driving" these bodies around. I guess what amazes me the most is that we all identify with them as being "us." And though they definitely serve a very useful purpose for various kinds of experiences, we are not limited just to the form we look like! Even when this body was fully functional and operating on the Earth plane, I <u>did</u> travel extensively without it. You remember how teachers would accuse me of daydreaming or not paying attention (who gives a darn about labeling?). Well, Sir, I'd been doing <u>that</u> since I could remember.

Ma, you know from your own experience as a teacher, the way little kids "leave" their bodies? Some just do it better and more often than others. And to think that this kind of traveling is being literally wiped out of existence by our educational society <u>today</u> in this country—it won't be that way for much longer. Anyway, got off on another track, didn't I? (smiling) Well, it just irritates me to see the way kids are treated nowadays for something that should be viewed as a gift rather than a curse! Or even worse—as something to be "corrected."

I know all the sacrifices you two (and many others) have been through with me in this state of being. But you also know that the "ripple" effect of all this is much more far-reaching than either of you can imagine. <u>Baba</u> knows—and you must never waiver in your faith in him. (Not that you would—you are like little crabs clipped on to the bottom of his robe—refusing to let go, no matter what the circumstance!) Just so you know, I get my daily share of *vibhuti* here before I begin any new projects.

Dad, I'm going to tell you a story. As you well know deep down inside, we've been together many, many times. No before (past) or future (after)—just now. We're replaying a <u>significant scene</u> (get it? actors on the stage)—you already know that. This is the scene of a lifetime. I will tell you a little bit about the history of this recurrent scene, which will explain <u>why</u> we keep replaying it together—with each other. In every other "lifetime" —all lifetimes ultimately wind up as one and the same and only "appear" different—you played the part of "the healer" (sometimes seen as a physician, medicine man, even shaman). Actually, we've <u>both</u> taken turns—one being the healer and the other one being the healed. You do understand, though, that this whole scenario is just an illusion for the benefit of the experiences we share with each other.

Okay, so it's your turn to be the healer—and please don't get me wrong. I <u>am</u> taking it all <u>very seriously</u>—I mean, look at the positions we're both in. (And, Mom, don't get too riled—I haven't gotten to you, yet.)

Dad, you've done and continue to do miraculous things—think just of how your own innate sense of faith and devotion has increased over the years. Also, consider your sense of commitment (always a tricky area, at best). <u>Yes</u>, take the credit for the wonderful and indeed <u>magical</u> way you've helped this ol' vehicle of mine. When people discounted your efforts and beliefs—you didn't let it get you down. Good for you! Another major hurdle overcome. "Damn the torpedoes and full speed ahead!"

But, also be aware that you are not <u>solely</u> responsible for the state of this body. Don't get me wrong here—I can't tell you <u>how much</u> I <u>appreciate</u> your dedication and help all these years—seriously. But, I guess what I <u>am</u> trying to get across is that if you "identify" with this role to the exclusion of everything else in life, that's a sure-fire guarantee that the play will continue to repeat itself.

What I'm trying to get across is that I don't want <u>you</u> to get entrapped in the role you are currently playing out—as you still see me entrapped in this sub-functional body. Don't you find it <u>ironic</u> that we're both trying to save the other from a fate we consider worse than death itself? And yet, it's our so-called "destiny," which determines these parts we play. And as everyone can see, we're <u>both</u> playing them for all they're worth. Your karma is inextricably tied up with mine, just as mine is intertwined with yours. Role after role, lifetime after lifetime, we keep working <u>so hard</u> at trying to "save" each other! Just think that over for a while!

So, the next question is, "save each other from what?" And you know the answer as well as I do—plain as day—we're trying to save each other <u>from</u> each other. It's a complicated scenario, but one we each find worth repeating, evidently. So, I just want you to know and <u>be aware</u> that through all the struggling and emotional upheavals associated with this so-called "dance" of ours, I so truly and deeply appreciate you. No other dad would have gone this "mile" that you have done.

But you must also be ready, when the time comes, to let it all go. I'm not saying that that time is near or far, but the process and acceptance of detachment (that Baba is constantly reminding us of) from the scene is every bit as important as the scene itself. Do you see what I'm saying? I mean, for instance, let's play the scene out two different ways.

Let's just suppose that one day the body all of a sudden repairs itself. All the work, stimulation, and sensation pays off big time, and I fully re-enter a functional body once more. After months of therapies of one kind or another, I am more or less ready to re-enter the world at large. Naturally, I want to live my own life, perhaps even to the point of doing stunts again. (Don't panic!) Think of how you would feel about all of that! Wouldn't you feel at a loss—even in a rage—that I go on my way eventually, leaving you in the dust? I'd be mad as hell (and have been) if I were in your shoes! What kind of karmic payback is that?!

Now take the second scenario: after years of hard work, dedication, and commitment on your part,

I just suddenly leave this ol' body for good—cut the cord and move on. On the outside, you'd be saying, "What a relief—for <u>all</u> of us, including Jay." But on the inside you'd be tormenting yourself as a failure and thinking that if you had just done "this" or "that" (or some combination), my body would have survived, perhaps even recovered. So again, there is the inevitable anger and resentment, turning in on itself, perpetuating the cycle. Reincarnation, pure and simple: <u>re</u> (again), <u>in</u> (in the), <u>car</u> (vehicle), <u>nation</u> (totality).

All I'm trying to say, Dad, is that detachment is as much a part of the experience as the experience itself. Don't worry or project into the future. Actually, neither of these scenarios will play out like this (exactly). I <u>am alive</u> and fully aware of each moment we spend together. Honest. But let's agree to "let it go" when the time occurs. Okay? What do you think?

I'm going to stop here and give this <u>patient</u> a rest. Will be back later (and I haven't gotten to you, yet, Ma). (smiling)

—Your Loving Jay

In this letter, Jay spoke about karma and spending many lifetimes in relationship with his dad. This letter definitely reinforced our feelings—which we had had all along to some extent—that the entire situation was a karmic lesson and that acceptance was one of the keys for "passing the course." Still, what Jay shared in this letter brought immense new dimensions to our understanding.

The following day, Wednesday, the fires in the area had been brought under control, and Jay did not have to move to another facility. We spent more time with him and met Elinor, the Feldenkrais practitioner who was working with Jay. Elinor also seemed to have an intuitive relationship with Jay; she seemed very in tune with him and had the sensitivity to pick up on his thoughts somewhat, a form of mental communication.

That afternoon, another letter came through Debbie, and in this letter Debbie at first had spelled Elinor's name as *E-l-e-a-n-o-r*, and Jay said to her, "want to spell it *E-l-i-n-o-r*," which was the correct spelling of her name. Of course, Debbie had not known this, as she was simply taking down Jay's dictation as she heard it. So this small detail was another "proof" that Jay inserted into this letter, to help us recognize the authenticity of what Debbie was receiving.

Jay spoke that afternoon about one of his co-inmates at the neuro-care facility and the frustration this coma patient was feeling with her husband and two sons. I did not include this section in the letter as it appears here, as it contained personal information about the patient and her family. I did read this part of the letter to her husband, and he wasn't sure if he could believe the information, so we left it at that.

LETTER 3

Wednesday, October 15, 1997, 3:30 p.m.
Tustin, California

D: Jay, it was really nice being with you today and seeing Eleanor work with you—also talking with Amanda and Brent [Jay's co-inmates], too.

J: Thank you <u>again</u> for coming all this way and spending time with me and the folks. I can't tell you in words how much this means to me! <u>All</u> the women in my life are special to me. I make it a point to be <u>with</u> them as much as possible. Girls like you, Ma, Jacqueline (the doctor), Amanda, Kim, and various ones who come in and out of my vision <u>are</u> important. It may make no sense at all to those of you who are running around like mad, "doing" things in life. But there is <u>noth-ing</u> that is wasted or unnecessary. People come in here to this facility all the time, feeling sorry for the patients, the families, the staff, themselves. It's unpleasant to be here—let's all admit that.

But, look deeper. As Swami Baba (how do you like <u>that</u> name) says, "dive deep" into the ocean. Look at all the "work" going on here. Look at the effects you are having on everyone who watches you. <u>Lots</u> of people—those <u>in</u> the body and many more who are not embodied—are <u>watching</u> you, learning from you, and experiencing the love, dedication, and faith that you exhibit when you come here. Don't you see that so many people are being affected and "blown away" by this whole drama! It <u>is</u> a divine play, no doubt about it—with S.B. directing from center stage. Literally <u>thousands</u> are being transformed (hard to believe, isn't it!?), by just hooking into the play.

You both <u>are living</u> and putting into practice the divine teachings from Baba himself, on a daily basis. It's ridiculous to think that all the intense and melodramatic stuff is happening in India or in other places where *vibhuti* and *amrita*[26] is manifesting. It's all happening right here, right in your own "back yard"—get it?!?

That's one of the main reasons I'm "busting my butt" to regain some amount of control of this body vehicle. It's like being in a badly smashed-up car and literally hammering out the dents one-by-one by hand. It takes lots of time, patience, and determination, but it's doable.

---

26 *Amrita* or "nectar of immortality"—the original ambrosia or "nectar of the Gods"—is an amber-colored, thick, honey-like liquid that may manifest as a sign of the presence of the Divine.

Instead of trying to aim at an "end goal," try to appreciate what's going on right <u>now</u>—at the moment. Yes, I'm going in-and-out of the form all the time—it can be a <u>real drag</u> at times, but the effect is worth it! Eleanor (want to spell it "E-l-i-n-o-r" . . .) can understand this; that's why we work well together. We exchange energies through the [Feldenkreis] exercises. The point I'm trying to make here is that you aren't "seeing" the subtleties of the entire drama. But, <u>instinctively</u>, you're doing all of the right things. The Gayatri every day (I say it too), the music, the *vibhuti*, the *lingam*,[27] the *lingam* water, the socializing, the laughter. All that's missing on a regular basis is the <u>singing</u>.

Okay, Mom, here's the drop . . . are you ready? (smiling)

I completely relate to your not seeing the body as <u>me</u>. Of course it's not me—never was! Yes, we're cute-looking on the outside and have our egos and identities all caught up with our looks. (Now, come on, you know we haven't let <u>that</u> one go entirely yet!) (smiling) Remember how much emphasis you placed on us looking "good"—especially

---

27 *lingam*, an ovoid-shaped object, similar to a stone, a mystical symbol that approximates the shape of creation—from the atom, to the solar system, to the universe; a *lingam* is a symbol of the Formless Absolute coming into form. Sai Baba has created numerous *linga*, some with very unusual properties.

at holiday and family events? And, darn it, there's a time and a place for that, too—it <u>is</u> important to look the part, which is why I always <u>love</u> dressing up in costume!

So, what's this all leading to? It's very, very important for you to see <u>beyond</u> the form, <u>beyond</u> the scene and stage props. That goes for everything, from this play here, to Puttaparthi and Swami. The <u>real</u> significance and the <u>real</u> gift and strength that you possess is your ability to <u>go</u> beyond the mundane, the trivial. And don't give me that look of "I'm just too tired anymore to keep this going." You haven't even begun yet. You're just warming up for the real production ahead of all of us.

I know, Ma, that you sorely miss all the joking and kidding we shared—I miss it too. But that's not the basis of our deep commitment to each other. You are my mother in this lifetime, and I am your son. We will never relinquish the roles, even after we're both long gone, because this earthly drama that is taking place right now is going to be viewed and reviewed an infinite number of times. We may have gone on to something else, but the energy of this particular time in earth's history will remain intact for eternity.

You still have a major part to play in Sai Baba's play; he hasn't made the move yet for you to see this. Why do you think you had to move, downscale, detach, live simply? You are a born leader and a born teacher. Swami has significant roles for you to play out, and I will be by you every step of the way. The time is not yet ripe for these elaborate plans to be put into action, but you can get a good idea of the direction they're going!

I know what you want from Sai Baba, but don't underestimate or shortchange your expectations (or his abilities!). You will truly be amazed at what he does in this and other worldly dramas. Your faith is strong, and it is strengthening daily with our experience together. But that's only a training period compared to what's coming "down the pike." Don't worry—it's something you can handle and will be so good at and for! Yes, you'll be pulled out of retirement. Think about it – re (again), tire (wheel of karma), ment (meant to be). All you're undergoing now is internal adjustments to your "in"-sight and outer perspectives, so that you'll be ready and prepared to carry on. Don't have a panic attack! There will be lots of people to help you in this new time, and for once you'll have the backing and support you need.

Yes, you'll go over to Swami's from time to time— but just for a family visit. He will be sweet, sweet, sweet to you (won't that be nice?). But he's a "tough guy" right now because he's toughening up a lot of devotees to be in shape for the times ahead. Can't have a lot of people "wimping out" on him in a crucial turning point. This also means a lot of "making your home" wherever you happen to be—not a permanent residence anywhere. Ma, you don't need any one place as permanent—too much of a hassle.

I'm going to stop here for now and let D take her break.

Okay, you guys, you know I love you <u>lots</u>. I'll still keep writing to you. Will nag D to come down again soon. Keep up all the good work, and don't you dare get depressed—I don't have time for that!

Love you!

—Jay

In this letter, Jay mentioned, "It's ridiculous to think that all the intense and melodramatic stuff is happening in India, or in other places where *vibhuti* and *amrita* (nectar) is manifesting. It's all happening right here . . . ." At that time, *vibhuti* had been manifesting under the glass of a photo in Jay's room, of Sai Baba holding up a golden lingam. Little dots of *vibhuti* began appearing here and there in the photo, and one day I was using a magnifying glass to look at these spots in different parts of the picture, when suddenly I saw *vibhuti* in the shape of a perfectly outlined cross, right on Swami's hand. I got very excited. The *vibhuti* built up for a while and then gradually disappeared. All that remains is a faint outline of the cross. The manifestation took place entirely under the glass, and we did not remove or disturb the glass.

Also, *amrita* (nectar) had formed on a framed picture of Jay and one of his buddies—a curved line of it, connecting Jay's image with that of his friend, in a garland or swag shape, leading from the right side of Jay's head, the spot where his injury occurred, to the right side of his friend's head. We found this interesting but can only speculate as to the meaning or symbolism of the *amrita*'s shape or position.

Another time, oil started to flow from a picture of Swami's feet that we have in Jay's room. This came to our attention one Sunday afternoon when a few Sai Baba devotees visited Jay and sang some devotional songs. While we were singing, one of the visitors noticed the oil coming off the picture.

Also, we had been given a *lingam* that Sai Baba had materialized for a friend of ours. When Baba made it, he told our friend that it was a healing lingam, and to pour water over it and give the water to people who were sick. This friend had since passed away, and she had given Jay the lingam. We pour water over the lingam and chant the Gayatri mantra while doing so; this is the water that Jay receives daily, and we also give away bottles of this "lingam water" to those who ask for it.

> *The* linga *is merely a symbol, a sign, an illustration—of the beginningless, the endless, the limitless—for it has no limbs, no face, no feet, no front or back, no beginning or end. Its shape is like the picture one imagines the Formless to be. In fact, linga means leeyathe (That in which all forms and names merge) and gamyathe (That toward which all names and forms are proceeding, to attain fulfillment). The linga is the fittest symbol of the all-pervasive, the all-knowing, the all-powerful.*
>
> —Sri Sathya Sai Baba[28]

---

28 http://www.srisathyasai.org.in/Pages/AshramInfo/Maha_Shivarathri.htm

These things were happening right in Jay's room, and he wanted to underscore to us that he was aware of it. Besides these spontaneous manifestations, if that's what one can call them, we have always chanted the Gayatri mantra daily and said prayers, as well as given Jay *vibhuti* and *lingam* water every day faithfully since the very beginning of this journey.

Also, I have always sung to Jay; I pretty much sing to him every day. For example, I will personalize the words to "O Danny Boy" and sing, "O Jay, Jay boy, I love you so . . . ." and adapt the words to the changing seasons, such as in the fall, "The summer's gone, and all the roses falling," or in the summer, "The summer's here, and all the roses blooming . . . ."

We found Jay's comments interesting and mystifying about so many people being transformed from hearing or "watching" this story unfold. I put a lot of thought into Jay's words on this, because he seemed to be talking about not only people here but people on the other side, and maybe even more so, the people on the other side.

He told us we need to see "beyond the form, beyond the scene and the stage props." This is perhaps another way of reminding us that his form or body is not the "real *him*"—and the same for all of us, that "we" are not the body, and that the things and events happening all around us are merely "scenery and stage props" for greater things going on.

This letter also contained quite a bit of what you might call predictive information. I didn't have much response to this. For one thing, I usually just do what I have to do in the moment and accept what comes up—whether it's a speaking invitation or a personal situation, and I honestly do not tend to think much about the future. We don't seem to have much control over what will happen anyway.

I have had psychic readings in the past, and anything like this that hints of the future, I tend to take with a grain of salt. I had to laugh, though, at the comment about "re-tire-ment"–_re (again)_, _tire (wheel of karma)_, _ment (meant to be)_—because Sai Baba had said to me previously in an interview, when I had thoughts about retiring from my position, "Retire? Don't tire."

Sai Baba has told us on many occasions and in various ways not to think about the past, not to think about the future, but to be and act in the present—the _omnipresent,_ as he says:

Man should not worry about what is past. The present is the product of the past. What has happened is beyond recall. It is futile to worry about the future because it is uncertain. Concern yourself only with the present. By "present," we may think it means only this moment. But this is not the present as Divinity sees it. For the Divine, "present" is what is "omnipresent."

—Sri Sathya Sai Baba[29]

*The present is both a product of the past and the seed for the future. If the present is properly taken care of, the future will be good of its own accord. Decide to do your duty in the present. It will pave a royal road for the future. **Duty is God. Work is worship**. Make these two mottos the guides for your*

---

29 *Sathya Sai Speaks* 21:25, Aug. 3, 1988.

life and pursue your studies in this spirit. If you are planning to do something in your future, what is the guarantee that such a time will come? Putting off obligations for tomorrow is irrational. Live in the present. Resolve to fulfill your immediate duties.

—Sri Sathya Sai Baba[30]

---

30 *Sathya Sai Speaks*, 20:17, July 30, 1987

CHAPTER 9

HOLIDAY SEASON, 1997

When we started receiving these letters from Jay in October 1997, I knew that the messages were pure and his words rang of truth, but I wondered where they were coming from, really? I had some doubts and didn't want to share the letters with others, especially with some of my family. However, I ventured to take the three earliest letters to a family reunion in Oklahoma in November 1997. All of us had graduated from a little ol' country high school called Alden, and we have an alumni gathering every other year, to which everyone who ever attended that little country school is invited.

Our family, the Joneses, usually sing at the alumni reunion, and we schedule a family reunion around our school reunion. By November 1997, we had received Jay's first three letters. Our family all stayed in the same motel; we usually met in someone's room, reminisced about the "old days," and shared food along with stories.

I decided to share Jay's letters with a few of my nieces whom I felt were open-minded. They were overwhelmed, and before we knew it, the letters were being passed around to the rest of the family. Everyone seemed to be inspired and to shed a few tears while reading them. Something was taking place on another level, and no judgment or even questions came forth—just a silence as the letters were read. All the family members seemed to resonate with the words in the messages.

Jay had always been the life of the party, and his cousins loved him dearly; now it was as if Jay were giving them spiritual advice, and they were listening and wanted more. It had been three years since his transitional experience, and overall they seemed to feel that he had finally broken his silence.

A couple of months later, in December 1997 and the first days of January 1998, we received four more letters from Jay, making a total of seven letters received within that short three-month period. When he wrote us on December 1, he called it his "Thanksgiving letter," and right in the first paragraph he mentioned "CNN," which Ron watched constantly on the TV in Jay's room, whenever he visited Jay (and still does). Perhaps this was another way of Jay's to convey to us his awareness of what is happening around him.

Then he started talking about how we weigh ourselves down mentally and create bondage for ourselves with desires and attachments, and how these mental patterns entrap us into a seemingly endless cycle of reincarnation. This part of the letter mirrors one of Sai Baba's frequent teachings comparing desires and attachments to "heavy luggage":

> *Desires must be gradually curtailed. . . .*
>
> *As desires multiply, attachment increases.*
>
> *This leads to more and more bondage.*
>
> *Bondage causes man to suffer in various*
>
> *ways. Where does bondage come from?*
>
> *Your own desires create your bondage. Your*
>
> *sorrows are your bondage. Reduce your*
>
> *desires and you will be peaceful. You will*
>
> *not face any danger. It will give you peace.*
>
> *Therefore, it is rightly said, "Less luggage,*
>
> *more comfort."*
>
> —Sri Sathya Sai Baba[31]

31 *Summer Showers 2002*, p. 156, May 24, 2002.

Later in this letter, Jay implies that his situation is a karmic obligation involving all our family that must be completed.

LETTER 4

December 1, 1997, 6:50 a.m. – 8:10 a.m.
Santa Rosa, CA

This is my Thanksgiving letter to you. I <u>tried</u> earlier on several occasions to come through, but this [Debbie] just happens to be a very busy "channel"! Like CNN, always something going on! Have to wedge myself in when the opportunity strikes, while the iron is hot. <u>Finally</u> was able to squeeze in this morning—so here goes . . .

It may not be apparent to you, entirely, to see the whole picture of what is happening where I am. Mostly, because you guys are still in the body "shell," bumping along—and, believe me, it's difficult to see much of anything with the limited physical restrictions of embodiment. Not that there aren't some pleasures associated with it, but it's a load to take in many ways. Hard to see what's right in front of you, even, when all you're doing is struggling to carry the load, right?

I mean, think about it like this: it's like packing a trailer full of stuff for a long journey, loading it up with all kinds of junk (because who knows <u>what</u> you might need <u>where</u>), and then finding out that you can't get up the hill ahead of you because there's too much weight in the vehicle, so what to do? Unload all the unnecessary "things" that are weighing the vehicle down—the things that are not useful right now. Like say, for instance, beach umbrellas, souvenirs, mementos, things from the past. You know that Swami is always saying, "Past is past; let it go." [He] says it here, too, all over the place. We're held back by our own thoughts, our memories of what was, what used to be, how "good" everything was at one time. Well, heck, it didn't seem "so good" at the particular time that it was happening—did it?

Just like now. You'll look back on this eventually and think "it was so good to do such-and-such, be at such-and-such place, doing such-and-such thing"—things you can't do at the moment you're thinking about them. This is how we get caught in thought—and make virtual prisons of our own minds. Even in the state of awareness I'm at here, we still do this same thing. I'm not immune from this kind of bondage either—it's a trap we all make for ourselves. All I'm trying to do is to point out the obvious.

We literally set ourselves up for the fall—and sooner or later, we finally get the point that it's only ourselves who ultimately learn to free ourselves from these mental traps. It's the desire, attach-ment, and constant repetition of the thought/habit-pattern of re-living experiences and mem-oirs, that bring us back again and again into phys-ical form. When we can honestly let go of—and by this I mean <u>truly release</u>, not just run away from or deny—each and every memory that we insist on replaying, then we'll all be making progress. It's like running the same video, over and over again, until the tape finally snaps—only in our cases, the tape doesn't wear out until we consciously push the "stop" button.

I'll bet you think I'm lecturing you guys, huh? Well, I'm not trying to sound like that, but these are some of the things that are going through my mind, and I want to share them with you.

This gal, Deb, is so funny. Do you know that she's drinking coffee and eating chocolate chip cook-ies for breakfast while we're doing this?!? My kind of gal! She thinks I'm squealing on her—ha, ha!

Anyway, this entrapment thing is a really impor-tant issue for all of us—which is why I bring it up. There you are, thinking that <u>I'm</u> trapped in-and-out of the body, and from my perspective, it's you guys who are more restricted and bound up. So we're <u>all</u> running around like mad trying to save and release each other, when we can't even save ourselves! Crazy, huh?! No wonder the Avatar of the Age had to appear now—we've all tangled ourselves up in so many knots that only someone of His Beingness could help us to untie our own knots.

And the significant point is that we have to untie our own knots ourselves—the very ones we've created over and over again for generations. Swami won't do it for us, but his grace helps us to keep on going, and working away when we would have given up long ago. So, as difficult and painful as it is for you to see my body in this condition (and me struggling, too, to keep it operational)—it's just as difficult and painful for me to see you guys in your bodies—struggling, processing, and moving forward inch-by-inch. From my viewpoint, I have much more "freedom of movement" than you, but I am compelled to stay close by until the karma of this situation with all of us is completed.

I do want to say, though, that as difficult and painful as these past several years have been for us all, it's also the closest we've ever been with each other! Think about it—I mean, we have been in touch virtually every day. How many people can say that? And your love, devotion, and sacrifice has helped all of us—and so many more beings that you're not even aware of—along our mutual pathways.

Think about it. Before any of this happened, it seemed like life was just humming along "naturally," when in reality it's not natural at all to be complacent. How do you like <u>that</u> word—one of my new ones! (smiling) Oh, I know, you were busy "working" —and it was work of a sort, but not the <u>inner work</u> that you're catching up on now.

It is a blessing for all of us to help each other like this—and so many others who are witnesses and active participants in this particular drama. It won't last forever; nothing does, and in some ways it will be a kind of relief and release when it's finished. But the main point to keep in mind is that it is our main opportunity <u>at present</u> to grow, to learn, to sacrifice, to embrace, and to love unconditionally—each other and ourselves—warts and all. We may not like what we see, but that's part of the whole process.

All of us are caught up in this fragile and delicate, yet so complex and beautiful dance with each other! We play our parts until the music stops and the curtain comes down, which isn't to say that we can't enjoy ourselves along the way—but enjoyment is not the ultimate objective or aim.

The sun rises here, just as it rises for you each day. And it sets, too, at the proper moment. Where I am, at the moment—in two worlds, so-to-speak— each moment is unbelievably precious, a treasure in itself. I can see and feel your moments of sadness and anguish, as vividly as you experience them, and I share in your moments of insight and joy. Don't give up on life—it is truly a gift from God that must not be squandered or taken for granted. There's <u>so much</u> that we assume "should be"— and we have no idea how much we are given.

The sun is rising in the heavens for all of us now. All we have to do is look toward it and appreciate the warmth, the beauty, and the life-giving properties it has to offer. I could have been a preacher, you know—it runs in my bloodline! Maybe next time around . . . . (smiling)

You know that I love you with all of my heart, and I so appreciate all that you do for me and all the rest of us here at the facility. Keep <u>moving</u>, and don't you get depressed on me, Ma. That makes me crazy! (smiling)

Love you guys! Give my love to everyone. Oh, by the way, everyone at the facility has tuned in on the "Swami channel"—they think Baba is really strange, but intriguing. Go around and do the Gayatri to everyone (quietly). Watch their reactions.

Love you lots!

—Your Loving Jay

It is hard to imagine the "other world" that Jay functions in, and his comments such as, "The sun rises here, just as it rises for you each day," and "I have much more 'freedom of movement' than you," only add to the mystery of his experience and his vantage point. It gives an added insight into the universal prayer from the Upanishads, "May all the worlds be happy." (*Samastha loka sukhino bhavantu.*)

Jay also mentioned, "I could have been a preacher, you know. It runs in my bloodline." This is a fact; Jay has three cousins and an uncle who were or are preachers. Not only that, but my sister, Vera, is an ordained minister, and, given the amount of teaching and speaking I have done over time in the Sai organization, I suppose I might qualify as a kind of "preacher" also.

On the last day of December we received another letter, where he addressed us as "Ma and Pa." These had been his favorite names for us, especially when he was being light-hearted and a little bit crazy—a small but significant detail that Debbie could not possibly have known about our family. For us, these little details that came through Debbie—Jay's tone, pet words, and his accurate references to things going on in our lives—were further signs that these letters were authentic and indeed from Jay.

In this next letter, Jay dwells a lot on the metaphor of "painting a picture" in life and in our relationships. To our surprise, around the same time, Debbie sent us a packet of pictures—paintings and artwork that she had "received" from Jay. One of these intriguing paintings is reproduced at the end of this letter. He wraps up his letter and the painting metaphor with a very beautiful Christmas message about living in the Will of God.

LETTER 5

December 31, 1997, 8:00 a.m. – 9:10 a.m.
Sonoma, CA

Dear Ma and Pa, Mom and Dad,

Good Morning! You're probably wondering why I said "Ma and Pa" and followed it with "Mom and Dad." Well, part of this letter to you is light, and part is serious. I mean, it's all serious, but some parts are more serious than others. (Now don't have a fit, Mom; you can handle this.)

I love this time of year—Christmas and New Year's. Christmas, because of the lights, festivity, excitement, anticipation, and close family bonding—and New Year's, because of the implication (my "word" of the week) (smile) of beginning with a fresh canvas, on which we can paint our yearly picture.

I always like the idea of having a "blank slate," whether it be symbolic or actual, on which to write, draw, or paint an entirely new scene. To me, it symbolizes the renewal of having another chance at creation. For instance, if you didn't particularly like the way last year's painting turned out, you can ditch it and start all over again! Isn't that great?!? ·

So, it doesn't matter if you made a mistake or just plain don't like your so-called "ugly" picture, because you have another chance to try all over again—using different brush strokes, other colors, another scene. That way, you don't feel too bad about the past painting and can ditch it in favor of starting something new and different.

Okay, Dad, I can hear you saying, "So, get to the point, what's this all about?!?"

(I have to switch pencils. Deb tried to write with one of those automatic jobs, thinking it would be a compromise between a regular pencil and a pen. It didn't work, so I'm encouraging her to go back to using a regular pencil—much better. Feels better too—stronger. We're battling over pencil versus pen, but I prefer the pencil—feels much more familiar to me. Thanks, Deb!)

Anyhow, to get back to the symbolic painting idea and the New Year: you know, Swami is always telling us (yes, here, too—and it's even more apparent and more clearly understood!) that each day, each moment, each and every thought we have is, in itself, a painting—a creation. One can paint beautiful scenes or one can paint dark, ominous, heavy pictures. We are the ones who choose the colors with which to paint the canvas.

God gives us the supplies, the illusion of time, and the idea to create a scene, a picture. But we have the option of choosing brilliant hues, pastels, or darkest pigments, with which we create our painting. Since we are all so closely connected, we can also influence each other on choices of colors and selection of pigments, which determine the nature of the scene—the "feeling" of the portrait we create. It's amazing to see what we are creating each day, each hour. Even the humblest of souls has the same God-given opportunity to create, to express, to experience the nature of the Higher Self in this way.

Even those of us who seem locked inside these physical vehicles are painting, creating, each moment of the day. The fact remains that most people don't see our creations, because they are running around so much that they don't stop long enough to really take a look at the wondrous pictures we paint. Though we move in a different mode than so-called "normally functioning" human beings—a much slower-paced mode than most of you around us—we are creating some absolutely, fantastically beautiful works of art that are appreciated by even the angels that cruise by!

It's very akin to some of the hand movements used by Tibetan Buddhists when they chant, only instead of hand movements, we express through color and dimension. Dad, you've seen, or at least felt, some of the work I've done, so you know what I'm talking about. In fact, we've done some pretty incredible "paintings" together! Thank you for being with me—hanging out with me—and working in such a dedicated, focused way. You'll soon see the amazing results of all these years of "investment." We've both grown tremendously from all your hard work and dedication, not to mention the effect that others have absorbed through this process. But don't let it go to your head, either—ha, ha! We're not here to be martyrs but simply very good friends.

I can hear you, Mom, thinking, "Well, what about me? You and Ron are having a good ol' time with each other, and I'm on the receiving end of a lot of grief! What kind of a deal is this?!"

Mom, everyone knows how hard this whole experience has been and still is for you. But you're still trying to hold on to something that was. Maybe you were feeling happier in the past—or thought you were—but we're all making tremendous strides and progress now. Now is where you need to be—not yesterday or even tomorrow. I'm not frustrated or miserable. In fact, I've never felt better! (smile)

You don't want to miss the boat on this one, Ma, because this is what your whole life is all about: being in this situation right now. Don't just resign yourself to it, or even surrender yourself to it; claim it for yourself, embrace it, love it, expand with it— you can do this—you must, because all of us depend upon it. We are all so closely intertwined with each other—and you and Jan must work together on this. It's the last piece to a very complex puzzle.

Baba knows it, and he is waiting for you to make your move. You know it, too, and it's real hard for you (we all know that), but you can do it! Heck, if I can do it, you can do it! (smile)

And you know what? As soon as you make that turn (and you'll know when that happens), we'll all turn together, and the pent-up energy associated with this situation will transform into bliss and will radiate through the realms of existence.

And don't whine about how it's always up to you to pull everything together in the end. You are my mother, and I know how strong you are! Why do you think I fought so hard to keep going in this body?!? I did have the chance at the time of the fall to exit, but my choice was to "hang in there"— like you've always taught—to reach the goal and help those around me. Heck, it would have been great to roam through the realms and travel all over, but I wanted to finish my painting with you, Dad, Jan, and all those around me whom I love.

So, what's all this leading up to? The end product of all of our creations, all our New Year's designs, becomes a singular product or scene of complete beingness—in which the all of every act, every situation, and every emotion, combines to form the One scene of complete radiance, complete love, and ever-expanding light that is reflected in the scene of the birth of Christ—that simple, humble, yet profoundly beautiful painting of the essence of creation.

The mother's love and sacrifice—the pain, discomfort, and yet total faith that God's creation would take place in the perfect spot—reflected by the light of the Star that so many beings were guided by. It wasn't her choice to give birth in a cave/stable, but it turned out to be perfect. Not only was Mary resigned, but truly grateful and excited at the prospect of living the Will of God.

"Not my will, but Thine." That's what all the sacred moments in time are all about—the true embracing of the Will of the One, of all that is. When we can let go, and paint our pictures with this in mind and heart, then our scenes on the canvas will be those of Holy Light expressed—expressed through us, again and again, unhindered by our own personal emotions or egos.

Thank you for bringing me home to spend time with everyone. Those moments are so precious for all of us. Have to go now; Deb is getting tired. Listen, you guys, I am right here with you. I love you so much; you are both the greatest!! Keep the faith—and fasten your seatbelts for an exciting year ahead. I'll be riding right next to you all the way.

—Your Loving Jay

In this letter, Jay said, "Heck, it would have been great to roam through the realms and travel all over, but I wanted to finish my 'painting' with you." By this he seemed to be saying he has some limitations as to how far from the "earth plane" he can travel in the spirit world—as if, although he's quite free to move about, he's "bound to a certain locale" to fulfill this role of functioning in a physical body as well as in an etheric form.

When the package arrived from Debbie containing a half dozen pieces of artwork, we were amazed. These, Debbie told us, were Jay's artwork—he had impressed upon her the concepts, media, images, and colors—complete with titles: "Coma: Through the World Darkly," "Eternal Flame," "For Dad," "This Little Light of Mine," and "Triple Incarnation." Apparently, Jay put Debbie's talents as an artist to work as an added form of communication. This was a different medium of message from Jay but no less profound.

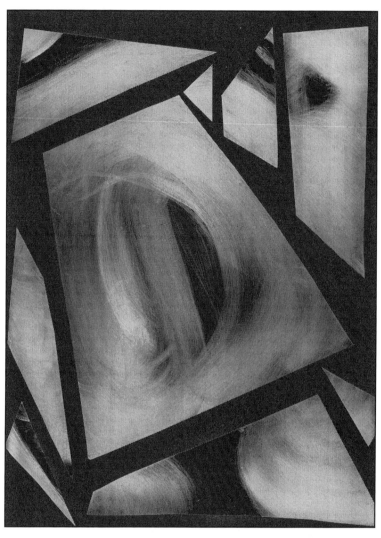

Coma: Through the World Darkly. Artwork by Jay Mead, 1997. All of Jay's paintings were done in color, including this piece. This is the only one, however, that came out well when translated into black and white, so it is the only one included here.

CHAPTER 10

PRIVATE LETTERS
TO EACH OF US

About the same time we received the paintings at the end of 1997, we also received a set of private letters the first week in January 1998. These letters were addressed to Ron, me, and Jan, separately, and they arrived in sealed envelopes.

In Ron's letter, Jay refers to Ron going through surgery. At the time, Ron had been diagnosed with bladder cancer and was getting ready for surgery.

Jay also tells his dad "not to worry about the smoking, for now." Ron had been addicted to nicotine, a smoker for over fifty years. He finally quit, five years later, when he was diagnosed with lung cancer in December 2002. Sai Baba cured his lung cancer in January 2003, and Ron has not smoked since that time.

LETTER 6 (PRIVATE LETTER TO RON)

*Saturday, January 3, 1998, 8:00 a.m. – 8:32 a.m.
Sonoma, CA*

Dear Dad,

This is a private letter to you from me. If you want to share it with Mom or others, that's up to you. You know as well as I do that Ma will <u>bug</u> you until you show it to her, but that's your choice (better you than me—ha, ha!).

You know, this is one of the craziest "dances" I've ever done—being *here, there, and every-where*—just like the Beatles' old song. But you've been with me on this insane journey through the darkness and the light—a sacrifice I will never forget. We both know how this drama is going to end (yes, you do), but we still have our own parts to play in it.

I'm glad you're still "in there fighting." You have to, because we've agreed to support each other until the time for release finally arrives. I just want to repeat to you how much I appreciate all that you've done for me and all that you do, even now, to "play the part."

Isn't it just hell having to take these worn-out bodies into surgery, just to keep them going? A big pain, if you ask me—worse than having to overhaul an old car—and lots more expensive! But it's our only mode of transportation at the moment, and we're stuck with them, whether we like it or not.

Don't worry about your impending surgery; I'll be there with you. You know what? We can probably go and have a good visit together while they're working on your body. What do you say? It'll give us a chance to catch up on things. So long as we don't go too far away, we can actually make a good time out of this, while we hang around "the body shop."

But our time in these ol' bodies is real limited, Dad; we both know it. I can't give you a definite time schedule, but I can tell you that time is limited for both of us. So, just a reminder to get your things in order—if you have anything that needs to be put in order. Drink the *lingam* water, and breathe deeply. We'll go through all this stuff together, just like we're doing now. Why do you think that blending our energies these past few years has been so important? Because we've always helped each other through the difficult moments in life. You've always been there for me, Dad, and I will always be here for you. I know I've said all this before, but I wanted to remind you of it all, because it's from my heart—no bull.

We both have to work with Ma to keep her up and moving. She's still got lots of work ahead <u>and</u> a book to write, too. I know she finds all this depressing, but she just has to get through it. We can and are helping her through it, but she still hasn't accepted a lot of it. You know the best thing to do for and with her, Dad, is to push her out of the doldrums. Take her down south for a couple of days to a nice place (yes, you can do that)—just the two of you. You'll be glad that you did. So will I.

Well, Dad, not much more I can tell you. I love you with all my heart. You're the best buddy and the best father in the whole world! Don't worry so much about me—I'm fine, and everything is on course. I won't let you down, Dad, so don't worry.

Looking forward to spending our time together soon. Give Mom a big hug and kiss for me—tell her I love her. And don't worry about the smoking—not a problem right now. You can deal with that one later. Tell Ma I said so—she'll <u>love</u> that one! (smiling)

See you soon. Hope you like the picture I did for you. I was "inspired"! (smiling)

—Your Loving Jay

One of the pieces of Jay's artwork that we received from Debbie was labeled "Dad" and looked like an abstract image of a face, so we figured that this was what Jay meant by the "picture" he had done for Ron. This image has two distinct horizontal rectangles in the area where the eyes would normally belong. Perhaps this image gives us an idea of how Jay's vision works. When my friend Mary Keane first looked at this painting, she burst into tears. She is an artist and saw right away that this was an impression of Ron's face. She pointed out how the two rectangles in relation to the face were in the exact position and shape of Ron's glasses, which have rectangular lenses. Not only that, the upper portion of the right "ear" of the face in the painting is bent, turned down, and the earlobe is lower than the left ear. Ron's right ear is "turned down" just like that, and is lower than the left ear. We doubt that Debbie—having met Ron only once—would have noticed such a detail. It seemed to us to be quite a definite portrait of Ron, close up, just as Jay's view of his dad's face would be when he is caring for him. And they do have a lot of "face time" together.

As mentioned previously, at the time we received this letter, Ron had been diagnosed with bladder cancer and was getting ready for surgery. The surgery was successful, and the bladder cancer has not returned.

The next letter was Jay's private New Year's message to me, in which he delivers some of the best "tough love" I've ever received. Though quite personal and directed to me, the advice Jay gives is applicable to anyone going through life's challenges.

LETTER 7 (PRIVATE LETTER TO BERNIECE)

Saturday, January 3, 1998, 9:45 a.m. – 10:50 a.m. Sonoma, CA

Dear Mom,

I know you're wondering <u>why</u> I'm sending "sealed" envelopes to you, Dad, and Jan. Well, here's the reason: I just wanted to tell each of you some very personal things, from me to you, which, if you wanted to keep them private, you could. You know that Dad and Jan will share their letters with you, and we don't have any secrets from each other. But you may choose to keep these letters to yourself—for now, anyway.

I've taken up a considerable amount of Deb's "free" time, because this opportunity won't come around again for me. You know what her life is like, and well, it's about to become even more busy! And my life is changing, too. You can see that 1998 is going to be a very condensed year, with lots of activity crammed in. A lot is going to be asked of each and every one of us, and we <u>all</u> have the wherewithal to complete our tasks. I aim to complete mine in the quickest, surest, possible way!

I know, Mom, you've always felt like the under-dog in a lot of your endeavors—not appre-ciated enough for all that you do, or even acknowledged. And don't tell me it doesn't mat-ter to you, when we <u>both</u> know that it does! Well, fasten your seatbelt, Ma, because you're about to become <u>real</u> acknowledged; just don't let it all go to your head! So, whatever depression, sorrow or sadness, self-pity, or negative "down" you may be experiencing—get rid of it. This is no time to feel <u>bad</u>. You haven't lost anything. Life wasn't better in the past, and the future <u>wouldn't</u> have been better if the fall had not happened in the first place. You keep insisting that life cheated you somehow—and there you are with the brass ring in your hand! I can't believe it! (smiling).

I know you don't want to hear this or read it, but by golly, Mom, I have to tell it to you. There you are with the blue ribbon in your hand, <u>first-place prize winner</u> of the spiritual lottery, the holder of the brass ring, and you're wondering why life doesn't treat you better?!

I'm not saying this isn't hard to go through. I wouldn't want to go through it in your shoes (or even mine), but it's our life plan, the reason we're here, our love of <u>being</u> that allows us to claim this as our experience.

I am fine. Dad is fine. Jan is fine. And so are you—you just don't believe it. It's not about accepting all of life's suffering as "God's Divine Will." This is a <u>gift</u>—to be here now—one that we've earned through many hardships and sacrifices, choosing love over hate, choosing love over sorrow, choosing love over hopelessness.

Don't let your mind convince you that this is a helpless situation. It's nothing of the kind. It is God's gift to us to be able to experience each other <u>just as we are</u>—perfect in every way.

If you see imperfection or feel rage over this, look inside you to see where it is coming from. I'm not trying to play psychologist here, Ma, or trying to play Swami; it's just crystal clear to me that you need to release some of this pent-up emotion and <u>look</u> at its origin, so that you can let it go. Think about it. Why would your life be the way it is, if you didn't need to have this situation in it in order to properly focus on the internal?

It isn't about Swami being the avatar of the Kali Yuga age or going to Puttaparthi to see God in human form; just take a look in the mirror if you want to see God in human form. Swami is present in our lives because we have all called him forth for guidance, facilitation, and to give us the experiences we need to <u>wake up</u>. Most of the nightmares in daily life are consciously accepted to prompt all of us to "awake."

Not a "wake"—we're already doing <u>that</u>. We need to "wake <u>up</u>"—get it? This is your prime opportunity to awaken, wake up, open your eyes, and take a good, long look around you. Nothing is lost; nothing is gained. The choice you have is either to wake up and expand, or stay asleep and contract. Now who's in the coma and who's awake? I'm sorry, Mom, to be so difficult—I'll bet you think I'm completely insensitive, but I'm not. I love you with all my heart, and because of this deep love for you as my mother and as my truest friend, I need to tell it to you straight. Shoot right from the hip! No trickery or cheating either! (smiling) This is not play-acting as a stunt would be, but as real as it gets.

I know where I'm going, and it's okay with me. You must never think that I'm gone, leaving you behind, rejecting, or abandoning you. Are you kidding me?!? I have <u>the best times</u> just being around you! But, Ma, you've got to grab, claim, and hold onto life's precious moments—each and every one of them. Don't let them slip through your fingers! Don't lose out on the present "feast" in front of you because you're too busy scrambling for the morsels of the past.

When things are seeming "down" to you—<u>sing</u>! Sing anything. I thought you were going to sing more for me—where is it? You've got a voice that even birds will stop to listen to. Don't let yourself get bogged down with heaviness. Get up, walk, sing, paint; do <u>anything</u> but dwell on sadness—it makes <u>me</u> crazy!

You know I love you completely. I <u>know</u> you can turn this around for yourself! I see Swami with you everywhere you go. How's that for a comforting thought? (Ha, ha!)

You don't have time to wallow in sadness. We're all going to be too busy for that. Do it next lifetime, if you must! (Ha, ha!) Life isn't meant to be seen as one of martyrdom. It's to be enjoyed, experienced, and <u>appreciated</u>.

I'm no philosopher, Mom, but from this unique perspective I've been given, I see <u>great</u> things ahead for you! And <u>lots</u> of things, so your current "holding pattern" is about to change. Get ready!

Love you, Ma. Love you, love you, love you. More walking and more singing—I want to see it and hear it, Ma. How's that for a demanding son? (smiling)

Give my love to everyone. I'm going for a walk with the dog. Oh, you wanted to know what the connection is/was between Deb and me? We've been very close friends and relatives through many lives together. In one life, I was her "eyes." Now she is my scribe—payback time, but we appreciate and enjoy each other's company!

Enough for now—<u>be good</u> to yourself!

—Your Loving Jay

At this time, I was again suffering with some bouts of depression, and Jay showed in his private letter to me that he was aware of this depression and addressed it. A "down" feeling would sometimes hit me out of the blue. I had been doing a lot of traveling, conducting the Sai Spiritual Education teacher trainings, and at times it got overwhelming for me. Sometimes it seemed that every flight I took, obstacles would crop up. People would be late meeting me, or my flight would be canceled and I would have to make arrangements for other flights. I would then entertain doubts about whether I should continue with this work, doubts that all too easily flooded my mind. I would wonder if I were being tested for my fortitude, or if should I take the obstacles and difficulties as signs to give up what I was doing. My mind would give me a sorry time indeed.

And, of course, I was constantly dealing with Jay's situation, and I kept thinking, "Why does this have to be so difficult?" We continually have to keep an eagle eye over Jay's caregivers, because mistakes and miscommunications can happen frequently. This letter helped me to come to terms with "all the situation" that I was dealing with at the time.

The following letter we received in a sealed envelope and mailed it to Jan in Wichita, Kansas. Sometime during the holiday period before we received these letters, Jan had asked Jay to prove the letters were authentic by "mentioning her name in one of them." Here, Jay writes her personally (and frequently mentions her name in future letters). In this letter, Jay acknowledges Jan's close inner affinity for Jesus, which was so— an inner resonation with the idea of Jesus, without feeling the necessity to be involved in a church. Jay also mentions two pictures of Jesus and "sent" them along with the letter. These pictures were not Jay's artwork but historic paintings of Jesus[32] that Jay had impressed Debbie to include, and he talks about these images as reflecting Jesus's inner nature.

---

32 One image was the Heinrich Hofmann painting, "Christ at Thirty-Three," showing Jesus gazing right, and the other was the face of Christ from "Temptation of Christ" by Titian (Tiziano Vecelli), showing Jesus gazing left.

LETTER 8 (PRIVATE LETTER TO JAN)

Saturday, January 3, 1998, 6:33 p.m. – 7:15 p.m.
Sonoma, CA

Dear Jan,

Yes, it's me writing this letter to you, whether you believe it or not! This is really so much fun—reminds me of all the times you and I would fight and argue over dumb little things: "I'm right!" "No, you're not!" "Yes, I am!" "No, you're not!" "You little _____ _____, yes, I am!" Remember? (How could you forget?) Seems like just yesterday, doesn't it? (smiling) Well, anyways, this isn't about all the times I was right and you were wrong—HA HA!!! Seriously, Jan, this will be one of the only times I get to write/ talk to you like this, and I have some things on my mind that I want you to know.

First of all, you <u>know</u> we're closer than bread is to butter, in spite of all our power struggles and disagreements. We still are and always will be. Don't let the sight of a dysfunctional body convince you that that's all there is left of me—far from it!! But I'm running all over the place and have lots of work I'm doing, so I don't just hang around 100% of the time waiting to regain more control of the body. Just keeping it going is a full time job! But I know and can see what's happening around me; let's talk about you.

How do you like the two Jesus pictures I sent? One you already have, I know (yes, you do—it's in one of your books). Well, you always wanted to know what he <u>really</u> looked like—these are as close as it gets. All the rest are mere approximations, but these reflect his inner nature.

Now the reason I'm sending these to you is because he's looking in two different directions—one to the right, the other to the left. If you hang these side by side on the wall, it will remind you that Jesus <u>himself</u> always had an open mind toward things and accepted everything as holy. Yes, even the so-called "bad" things, he transformed into sacred and pure.

Jan, don't let life pass you by as you hold on to just a few ideas as "right" and throw everything else away. You're too bright for that! Give yourself a break—lighten up—life isn't as bad as you think it is. You've only boxed yourself into a corner and can't see the way out. There's so much inside of you just waiting to be released—all kinds of wonderful things, beautiful things. Let go—just a little—and you'll see what I mean. Nothing bad will happen to you; all you have to do is open up a little, take a chance, let some of that divine happiness <u>out</u>. Laugh more—you're taking all of this way too seriously—not good for your health. Just be happy a little more and let go a little more.

You don't have to go radical, shave your head, and beat a tambourine (man, Mom will go crazy if she reads this). Your potential inside is limitless, and you've got more than enough to go around, plus some. You don't have to get into it with the folks about Sai Baba or any other kind of "Baba"; stay with Jesus, because that's where you are— they'll understand, and so will you. It's not about whose teacher is better, but what you're doing with yourself that counts! Heck, I can see your light shining way over here, so I <u>know</u> it's there—let it out! See, I haven't changed—am <u>still</u> telling you what to do, ha, ha. The pictures are from me—the message I'm giving you is in the two pictures I'm sending you.

I miss our times together, Jan, but I'm still keeping an eye on you—no mistake about that! I'm happy, healthy, and fully mobile from where I am, so don't go feeling bad or guilty about seeing me or not seeing me. I can see <u>you</u>—and what I want to see more of is you laughing, smiling, letting go, and loving more. You can do this—don't hold back so much. And also let your husband be "right" once in a while (even if he isn't)—cut <u>him</u> some slack. He's a great guy—be good to him.

And don't think I won't be watching, 'cause I will! Always am! Play more with the kids—become more of a teacher. You come from a long line of <u>great</u> teachers! It's in the blood. Find your peace, Jan; the Lord will guide you if you only ask for it. I ought to know!

You're a wonderful person, Jan. You only have to believe in yourself. I believe in you already, and that's saying something, being as I'm your brother—through thick and thin!

Love you, Jan—always have, always will!

Your loving brother, Jay

P.S. If you <u>still</u> don't think this is from me, then who do you <u>think</u> it's from???

Love ya, J.

Although this was the only letter from Jay over these years that was formally addressed to Jan, she has always felt close to him since his "transition experience." Jan used to call Jay by the nickname, "Jay-bird." During the first couple of months that Jay was in a coma, she would come across blue jay feathers just about every time she went outdoors, and she felt this was a sign from Jay. Since that time, when she thinks of Jay, she finds blue jay feathers "in her path." Also, from time to time, Jay has come to Jan in her dreams and given her messages.

Despite these comforting events, Jan has found that grief over Jay can surface at any time, even many years later, and can be triggered by many things, such as health challenges involving Jay, Ron, or myself—or even through reminiscences or friends of Jay's who sometimes surface from the past. Jan set up a web page for Jay, and sometimes people contact her through that means. Also, our grandson, Nathan, had had wonderful times with Jay from the earliest age, and had idolized his Uncle Jay, who loved to horse around and was such fun as a "pal"—and the change in Jay's status had been difficult for Nathan as well. So, sometimes grief is an ongoing phenomenon.

Near the end of Jan's letter, Jay advises her to "become more of a teacher." Interestingly, the next fall, Jan began taking college classes, gradually working toward a degree. She thrived on research and participated in some significant research studies as an undergraduate, then determined to continue toward a master's degree and doctorate, with the goal of teaching at the college level.

൦൦

Just as the joy felt in dreams disappears when you wake, the joy felt in the waking stage disappears when you wake into the higher awareness, called jnana (knowledge). So, the Upanishads say, "Get up, arise, awake!" Time is fleeing fast. Use the moment while it is available, for the best of uses, the awareness of the Divine in all.

—Sri Sathya Sai Baba[33]

---

33 *Sathya Sai Speaks* 5:14, March 26, 1965.

CHAPTER 11

MORE LETTERS AFTER A LONG SILENCE

It would be six long years before we would hear from Jay again. During the intervening years, besides caring for Jay, I continued my travels training new and continuing spiritual education teachers for the USA Sai organization. Ron stayed home, as he was very busy with Jay's affairs. As Jay's conservator, Ron is responsible for Jay's health and estate, and in dealings with the court system. We also have found that since Jay cannot talk for himself, he receives better care when we make constant, regular, and frequent appearances at the facility—several times a day, if at all possible.

Our home is only three miles from Jay's residential care facility. Ron and I have worked out a system whereby Ron goes to the facility in the morning for two or three hours; I go in the afternoon, and then we both return at Jay's bedtime to have a prayer and to have contact with the night shift of nurses and aides. This has proved to be the most successful method in Jay's case, to communicate with the staff and closely monitor the care he is receiving. Ron continues to work daily with the nurses and therapists, training them when needed, and when new or temporary staff members come and go, so that Jay receives the best possible care.

During 1997 or 1998, sometime after my trip to India when Sai Baba talked about Jay having essentially only a mind and not much body function (*"Mind is everything; mind is everywhere. Mind is all he has—he has no body . . . body not good."*), we hired a neurosurgeon for an evaluation. We went to a great deal of effort to bring Jay to this doctor's office, and because Jay's body can only go so long without receiving water, we were on a very limited time schedule. But despite the fact that no other patients were in the waiting room, this doctor made us wait for over an hour. When a sales rep showed up after we had arrived, the doctor met with the sales rep. We wondered if we were invisible or something. I had a strong feeling that this fellow did not have his priorities straight and felt like leaving right then, but since we had already paid for this consultation, we decided to see it through, even though it went against our intuition.

Finally, after looking at Jay and examining a CT scan that showed no more damage had happened to Jay's brain but also no more improvement, this doctor advised us, "He has no mind; all he has is a body." This was the exact opposite of Baba's statement. At these words, Jay began to fidget and cough emphatically. This neurosurgeon went on speaking as if Jay were completely unable to hear or understand our conversation. He even went so far as to tell us that if Jay were to get pneumonia, it would be best not to give him any treatments and to "just let him go"—in other words, let him pass away.

After we left that doctor's office, I reassured Jay, "Don't worry, we are not about to listen to that doctor!"

JAY BREAKS HIS SILENCE

On December 27, 2004, we received our ninth letter from Jay. We hadn't heard from him in this manner since January 3, 1998. One of our acquaintances had commented to us, "These letters (from Jay) have layers and layers of personal and spiritual meaning. You can't absorb them all at once." He speculated that perhaps Jay was waiting until we had assimilated and put into practice some of the suggestions from the previous letters, before communicating with us again. Regardless of the rhyme or reason, we were of course very happy to have another communication from Jay. Again, we have never asked Debbie to contact him, and we wait entirely for the messages to come without our prompting.

Jay jokes with us at the beginning of this letter about "the wink of an eye," making a point to emphasize "wink, not *blink*," which was another way of letting us know how aware he is. "Blinking" is one of the ways Jay communicates with us, using his physical abilities. To respond to a question, we ask him to blink his eyes—and he does.

Jay discusses the challenges of a coma patient in responding to other people in the physical world. In this regard, Jay has come very close to—if not actually—expressing words at times. One time at Jay's residence facility, an aide, the cook, and the activity director were with him and talking to him. Jay began coughing, and they asked him, "Are you okay?" Jay coughed really hard, and out came the emphatic sounds, **"I'm okay!"** All three of them heard it clearly. Apparently, Jay was able to approximate these words, with great effort, through the explosive energy of a cough—a way to get around the use of some of the throat and voice box muscles that have been affected by the state of the brain. This happened another time, too, when an aide was putting Jay in bed, and Jay again coughed strongly to create the audible statement, **"Okay!"** I have also heard Jay whisper quite clearly, "Hi!"

Jay also mentions in this letter the song, "This Little Light of Mine," which was also the title of a piece of artwork we received from him at the end of 1997.

LETTER 9

December 27, 2004, 10:30 a.m. – 2:08 p.m.
Santa Rosa, CA

Hey Mom and Dad!!!

Bet you wondered if you'd ever hear from me again like this, right?!? Seems like a long time since the last letters, but you know in your hearts it's just the wink of an eye (get it? <u>wink</u>, not <u>blink</u>? ha, ha!). See, I haven't lost my sense of humor, either. Love to Jan, et al, too, in case she thinks I've forgotten about her. Not a chance there, either. You guys are always, <u>always</u> in my thoughts and heart—you know that.

Okay, so you're probably wondering what I've been up to in the span of earthly years that have passed by. Well, I've been <u>busy</u>, that's what. (No surprise there.) But before I go into that, a couple of things I want to tell you both. First of all, Dad, you are something else! What can I say?!? All these years of taking care of me—how can I ever tell you how much that means? I know, I'm using a lot of expletives, but I'm <u>so</u> <u>excited</u> to be able to tell you what's going on, and I feel a sense of urgency at getting all my thoughts and feelings expressed to you.

Anyway, Dad, I <u>know</u> everything you do for me, <u>feel</u> it all—yes, I'm present enough to know when you're due here to care for this big, ol' body every day. And, though most people don't understand this, the body vehicles are just as important to those of us in comas as they are to you. We simply move and respond A WHOLE LOT SLOWER than the rest of the world. But we <u>do</u> move and we do <u>respond.</u>

Some of us are slower than others. It took me a long time to adjust to this, even accept it, but there are moments of breakthrough when we can elicit responses that are obvious enough and explosive enough (and <u>quick</u> enough) for you guys to pick up on.

It takes an incredible amount of energy on our parts—and some planning ahead—to respond at a high enough level for you all to see and hear. For us, it's the equivalent of an Olympic feat— and it takes enormous discipline, build-up, and focus. And then we have to literally "jump" when that window of opportunity presents itself. We can see it coming—kind of like the brass ring of a merry-go-round (I wanted to say *carousel*, but Deb put *merry-go-round*)—and most of the time it seems like it's out of reach for many of us who are immobilized.

Also, there's a large factor of unceasing support, love, and stimulation that, if not provided by family and loved ones, is needed to help the body maintain function. You both have been <u>incredible</u> for me and to me. You can't possibly see or imagine the far-reaching effects your devotion has had on hundreds and <u>thousands</u> of people! Not just where you are, but also on the planes you don't see. I'm always showing people here what you're doing, where you're going—and even <u>they</u> can't believe it.

So, Dad, I'm glad you decided to stick around for a while longer—<u>ha, ha</u>. See how we all affect each other?! You don't think Sai Baba's going to let you off the hook that "easy," do you? Just kidding, Dad!

Actually, we all made a lot of strong appeals to the "head man" on your behalf, Dad, and made some really good arguments, too. Truth is, you were willing to make some significant changes, and your "good karma" account was plenty full to allow a withdrawal. It's a _lot_ harder to stay in the world than to leave it—and you're talkin' to one who knows! Good move, Dad; now just keep an eye on your vision, kidneys, and gut. Nothing alarming—just check in on these areas from time to time.

Dad, you're the greatest! Don't worry about living on borrowed time—we're <u>all</u> living on borrowed time. Ain't ours to control, anyway—never was, never will be. Honestly, we are—each and every one of us—here by the grace of God, simple as that. Every moment is a moment of grace, no matter how we see it. And every conscious moment is an opportunity to serve, whether we see it not.

See, we, as souls, receive the divine energy, or grace, so we can then serve others—pass it along, keep the divine in motion. Get it? **Grace is love in motion**, and that's how this whole universe works and keeps on unfolding, changing. There's no inherent good or bad to what happens, just plenty of opportunities to stop focusing so much on ourselves and instead reach out to others, especially when they ask for help.

That's what you always taught us, Mom—the Golden Rule—remember?!? And "This little light of mine, I'm gonna let it shine. . . ."? Well, we sing it where I am as, **"This little light of Thine, we're gonna make it shine. . . !"** Isn't that great? "Thine" meaning the grace of the Almighty Source of Light inside all of us. Sorry if I sound "preachy," but it's <u>so</u> obvious from where we are.

Okay, Ma; you're the one on the hot seat now. How's thing's going? I know you've had to slow down a bit recently—gotta put those feet up more. It's a drag to be immobilized, don't you think?! Still, we have to listen to these hi-tech vehicles if we want to keep driving them around town!

How's your book coming, Mom? Has Swami talked to you about it yet? From my perspective, here, seems like the kids growing up today are getting hooked into electronics more and more, speeding up their brains but not their hearts. We need to return to basic simplicity of family life—like family dinners, playing, joking, conversations, and personal communication. From here, it even looks like relationships are between individuals and their machines, rather than individuals with each other. I mean, what's the point? And where does this put God?!

This probably won't be a popular topic with your audiences, Mom, but it has to be said. Divinity can't be found in a laptop or an iPod.

(Debbie took a break here. Time: 11:40 a.m. Resumed note-taking at 1:00 p.m.)

Speaking of vehicles, I had to let Deb here take a break, so we could continue now at full speed!

Mom, you're often wondering just where the heck I am, right? Well, I haven't gone anywhere! Surprise, surprise!! I'm right where I've always been—here. Actually, I still have a "leg" in both realities—the earthly realm and the more extended conscious realm where I do most of my "work."

Right here. I don't have to "go" anywhere—there's no need. You don't go, you simply are where you find yourself. Same thing where you are, except you do it in conjunction with a physical body. So, I don't have to go to a war-torn part of the world to help those in need; they come to where I am, in consciousness. The people—that is, men, women, children, and teenagers (even teenagers!)— arrive on the scene here, where I spend most of my time. Just joking about the teenagers!! I can say that because they're the group I happen to like working with the most.

Most—the majority of people I help on my end of things—are those who suddenly find themselves in another "land" or twilight realm. From trauma, shock, a sudden injury, or an accident that results in immobilization of or loss of their bodies, they very often find themselves in a semi-darkness, where things are not seen clearly. Truthfully, this is a temporary state, in-between states of awareness, allowing that person "time and space" for adjusting, adapting, and accepting what's happened to them.

I'm one of many working on this "AAA" team—as a counselor, if you want to see it that way, or a "travel agent," as I often call myself. More people relate to "AAA travel agent" than to "guide," "counselor," or "advisor." My job is to keep 'em moving and get them to their destination, whether that be back to driving in a physical form (returning to their bodies) or taking the fast track to heaven.

I prefer working with the teenagers because their sense of rebelliousness is at an all-time high—not that I can relate to that!! (smile) They're the group with the most questions, the highest sense of adventure, and the most attitude. They also have the highest rate of return to their physical bodies of any age group.

So, to make a long story even longer, from everywhere and anywhere in the world, when a disaster strikes, we have an immediate influx of people here. Immediate! They're often confused, angry, upset, freaked out, and frightened. What we do is just exactly what you guys are doing where you are: we sit with them, help them, answer questions, walk with them, explain their situations to them, listen to them, and wait with them—until they are ready for the next part of their journey.

Do we ever get tired of this work? Well, I admit I have to sometimes take a break now and then, but for the most part, each person is different. And we see the world through *their* eyes, *with* them, so we experience everything that they do, see, and feel. Eventually, just as on the earth plane, they become strong enough to continue their journey without the extra support from us.

And yet, a part of us goes with them, continues on with them. As you are helping me, I am able to help them, and they go on eventually to help others. A piece of us moves on with each person, each living thing that we come into contact with. This is what I mean by love in motion—or you could say divinity in action; the light keeps growing and glowing.

So many kids here wonder why life on earth is considered to be so important, so valuable, when they see war, devastation, greed, hate, and death all around. Well, from here it's perfectly crystal clear why life on planet earth is sacred, above all. It's the place where extremes are pushed to the max, where separation (or at least the illusion of isolation) is the strongest felt, where ego is allowed the most temptations, and where experience allows the greatest and quickest transformations possible within such a short period of time. The most "bang" for the buck:

"You always get your money's worth on challenging, adventurous planet earth!"

Like that phrase? It's part of my "spiel" for the kids who come here and wind up returning to their bodies.

Okay, folks, that's it for now. I <u>love</u> you guys—always remember that!! And be good to yourselves—that goes <u>double</u> for Jan! I'd tell you that I miss you, but truthfully, I'm always with and around you—always under your feet!—Ha, ha! Some kids just <u>never</u> grow up! That's me, I guess!! (smile)

Love, Love, Love,
—Jay

In this letter, Jay dwelt on the value of a human life and how we're all here by the grace of God, living on "borrowed time." He mentioned that he was "glad that Dad could stick around a little big longer." Ron had survived several serious health issues: he had come through heart surgery the year before, in September 2003, and Sai Baba had cured Ron of lung cancer prior to that, in January 2003. Ron had also survived bladder cancer and a bout of septicemia within the previous few years.

Also, two of my brothers passed away during 2004, one of them on Christmas Eve, just three days before this letter arrived from Jay. All this brought up for me how fragile our human lives really are. Sai Baba often reminds us that this life is like a water bubble; it can pop at any time:

> *Human life lasts but a moment; it is a*
>
> *bubble on the waters. Upon this ephemeral*
>
> *bubble of life, people build for themselves*
>
> *a structure of desires and attachments.*
>
> *Wisdom warns that it might collapse or*
>
> *crumble any moment.*
>
> —Sri Sathya Sai Baba[34]

In a related vein, Jay also discussed the work he does when a disaster strikes on earth and great

---

34 *Sutra Vahini*, ch. 4, p. 35

numbers of people leave their physical bodies at the same time. We felt this was probably an indirect allusion to the tsunami that had taken place the day before, on December 26, 2004, in Southeast Asia, which had caused massive destruction and "loss of life" in that oceanic region. Maybe this was what he meant when he emphasized, "I've been busy!" He shared that when many people leave their bodies during a disaster, individuals like himself (coma patients who have not yet left their bodies entirely) or other helpers in the spirit world or earth plane, help out with those making their transition from the earth plane into spirit. Apparently, the newly-crossed-over individuals are often disoriented, angry, upset, and frightened. Jay described how he and others work with these souls in the "more extended conscious realm," as he called it, humorously referring to his job as like an "AAA travel agent."

Jay also mentioned to me about having to slow down a bit lately and put my feet up. In fact I had had knee surgery the previous January. He also talked about the challenges, as a coma patient, of making visible responses to those who visit or care for him, and how he is aware of and viewing visitors and caregivers from a more expanded level. He mentioned being able to "see" the opportunity coming but not always being able to make the body respond in time to be noticed.

In this letter, Jay asked again about my "book," but I still couldn't see it happening. And no, Sai Baba had not said anything to me about a book—yet. But those with whom we shared the letters often asked for the letters to be made into a book.

ᘒ

The play is His; the role is His gift; the lines are written by Him; He directs; He decides the costumes and props, the gesture and the tone, the entrance and the exit. You have to act well the part and receive his approbation when the curtain falls. Earn by your efficiency and enthusiasm to play higher and higher roles—that is the meaning and purpose of life.

—Sri Sathya Sai Baba[35]

35 Quoted in *Sai Baba: The Holy Man and the Psychiatrist* (San Diego, CA: Birth Day Publishing, 1975), pp. 189-190.

CHAPTER 12

THE HUMAN BEING: A SOPHISTICATED TUNER-AMPLIFIER

There is current in the human body from

top to toe. The body itself is a big generator.

Illumination Mind, which is related to the

current in the body, is very powerful. . . .

The thoughts, words, and deeds of one with

Illumination Mind are suffused with divinity.

That gives rise to a very powerful "three-

phase" current in the body. . . . Just as a

generator can illumine a bulb connected to it

> *even at a distance of 100 miles, likewise the*
>
> *current originating from the sacred feelings*
>
> *in the heart can travel up to any distance.*
>
> *This is the power of Illumination Mind.*
>
> —Sri Sathya Sai Baba[36]

On April 7, 2005, we received a call early in the morning saying that Jay was experiencing seizures, and that the staff at his neuro-care residence had called the paramedics to take Jay to the emergency room at the hospital. By the time we reached the neuro-care facility, the paramedics were putting Jay into the ambulance, and he was still having seizures. I asked if I could ride alongside Jay in the back of the ambulance, but they told me that they would be too busy and that I would be in the way. They did, however, allow me to ride in the passenger seat of the ambulance.

I had in mind putting his lingam on his forehead, which was why I wanted to sit right next to him in

---

36 *Sathya Sai Speaks* 33:19, Nov. 20, 2000. This discourse discusses various levels of mind: super mind (related to body consciousness), higher mind, illumination mind, and over-mind.

the ambulance. Jay has a twitching in his eye on occasion, and when we place the lingam on his eye, it stops twitching. I had a lot of confidence that this would also stop his seizures. But I was not successful in getting this message across to the paramedics, who looked at me as if I were a little bit crazy.

Then, when we arrived at the hospital, the hospital personnel would not let me go into the room with Jay at first. I felt frustrated, but all I could do was just accept the situation for what it was, and pray and hope that I could be with Jay, if this were to be his time to give up the body vehicle. Ron drove over separately to the hospital, joining us later.

After about an hour in the ER—Jay had been having seizures for three hours by this time—they finally let me into the room. He looked so frail and pitiful. They had cut away nearly all his clothes. His head was bent backward, and he was moaning, with his body still convulsing. I could tell he was frightened. I started talking to him and immediately placed the lingam against his forehead. I began singing the Gayatri mantra—Om Bhur Bhuva Suvaha . . . , and Jay began to settle down. Within a minute or two, his seizures stopped completely. Somehow the medical personnel stepped aside and let me do this. By this time, I'm sure they had given up and felt that he was not going to make it anyway. Then, all of a sudden, the electricity went off, and the room was plunged into total darkness. I had a feeling this had to do with the power of the lingam.

We heard shouts of "don't panic . . . the generator will kick in very soon." Soon the lights came back on, and Jay appeared calm but deeply comatose. They took him for a CT-scan and found that he had not suffered any further brain damage. Jay had been over-medicated in an effort to stop the seizures, and this had induced him unintentionally into a deeper coma. As a result, he had to be placed on a ventilator for a few days. He spent nine days in the intensive care unit under these conditions, until he could regain the ability to breathe independently.[37]

That year, a series of public meetings had been scheduled across the country to present information about Sri Sathya Sai Baba and his many social works—the free and loving, charitable, educational, and health care programs that have been Sai Baba's outright gifts to humanity. I had been invited to speak at one of these public meetings, in Hartford, Connecticut, on Saturday, April 16. I had plane

---

37 Jay's usual level of coma has been referred to as level "3-4." Lower numbers on the scale mean a lower level of functioning, so being unable to breathe on his own took him below "3" on this particular coma scale.

reservations to fly there that Thursday, but I did not feel like leaving while Jay was still in the ICU. Ron, however, encouraged me to go, as I had obligated myself to be a speaker, and they were expecting me. So I decided to go.

I stopped by the hospital before my flight and told Jay where I was going and that I would be back very soon. I still felt very reluctant and sad about leaving, my heart torn between seemingly competing obligations. At the airport, at the last second, I decided to call Ron before boarding my flight. Wonder of wonders! I could hardly believe it when Ron told me that Jay was being taken off the ventilator and would probably get to go back to his care facility on the following Saturday, only two days later. I was so happy at this unexpected news that I broke down and cried. I felt total gratitude to God for this miraculous resolution, which freed up my heart, just when it was needed most—and in Sai Baba's signature style, at the last second and not a moment sooner. He tells us, "Love my uncertainty."

> *You must have freedom not only from*
> *fear but from hope and expectation. Trust in*
> *my wisdom. I do not make mistakes. Love my*
> *uncertainty, for it is not a mistake. It is my*
> *intent and will. Remember, nothing happens*
> *without my will.*
>
> —Sri Sathya Sai Baba[38]

My good friends, Jay and Merle Borden, met me at the airport in Connecticut and took wonderful care of me over the weekend. The public meeting was successful, and I was able to follow through on my given word, fulfilling my obligation to the organization. When I returned home, I found Jay looking very good. They had started him on a different seizure medication, which was working for him. Jay did not suffer any other seizures until September 2009. We were very lucky and grateful for this period of relative stability—as a seizure crisis can easily become a mortal crisis.

---

38 *Sanathana Sarathi,* August 1984 (monthly publication of Sri Sathya Sai Books & Publications Trust, Prasanthi Nilayam, India). All but the first sentence also appears as end quote in *Sathya Sai Speaks* 30:31, after discourse of Nov. 22, 1997.

I was kept very busy throughout 2006, and Jay remained stable, which made all the travel much easier for me. Then, after a silence of almost exactly two years without any letters from Jay, we had a surprise that started 2007 off on a happy note, literally. On January 5, 2007, we received another letter conveying more spiritual insights.

In this long letter, Jay makes an analogy about feeling like he's "running a marathon in mud," when it comes to getting his physical body working more efficiently, compared with all the work he's doing in the "more extended conscious realm," as he has referred to the spiritual dimension where he is. He lets us know that he knows that Ron and I often feel this way too, as if we're making very little progress for all the effort put into his care, or when having to rise above our own physical issues and discomforts to carry out all our many commitments.

Then he launches into a breathtaking metaphysical lesson on the purpose of life—using a very scientific analogy of the human body being like a sophisticated "tuner/amplifier/transmitter." Again, he points up how he has a "leg in each world"—experiencing life in a physical body as well as being free to travel around in what might be called the astral or etheric plane.

LETTER 10

January 5, 2007, 2:38 p.m. – 4:29 p.m.

Hi Ma and Pa,

Well, here I am, writing you again through this most amazing method of communication, don't you think? How are you guys <u>doing</u>? Of course, I know the answer to that, since I see you every day, but I don't want you to think I've lost my manners or sense of humor!

Debbie, here, has been under the weather with some kind of a bug—but is feeling well enough to take down some of my thoughts to send off to you. I've been buggin' her for weeks now (could you feel my vibes, Debbie?), but you know how busy life can get "on the outside," especially around the holiday time of year. Anyway, I've got a lot of things on my mind to say to you all. (Yes, Jan, that means you, too.) So, here goes . . . .

You probably want to know how I'm feeling, what I'm doing, and what's going on in my neck of the woods. I sure wish I could get that ol' body functioning and cooperating a bit better, so I could tell you directly (I am still working on that). As you've probably guessed, I'm REALLY busy most of the time. It's like running a marathon in mud—sound familiar? I work a lot with groups of kids, and one-on-one with emotionally troubled kids (both here and there), and head up a men's interaction group. I know this may surprise you, but there are a lot of guys over here, too, who are really confused and disoriented when they figure out what's happened to them—especially those who are both here and there, similar to my position. And also work with a lot of the people who are around me all day long here.

And I also spend time with you all every day, too, and not just in the residence facility. A guy likes to get out once in a while, too, you know! (Ha, ha!) Seriously, though, I cannot begin to tell you how important the work is that you're doing with everybody, and especially all the incredible support you've given me all these years! I know it must seem to others like we're being held captive in these bodies of ours—especially when someone is in a condition like mine or confined due to illness. And what I want to try to convey this time around is the actuality of what is really happening.

You know what these physical bodies of ours really are? They're very sophisticated amplifiers. Yep, that's what they are—electronic sound systems. Isn't that a hoot? Some are louder than others, right? And some you just wish you could turn off for long periods of time. (Ha, ha!) And then, sometimes the wiring just gets all screwed up, and that affects the quality of the sound and the distortion coming out. But when you come right down to it, these hunks of flesh, operating under a complex set of programs, are "driven" by electrical fields and signals that they both attract and repel. It's simple physics—or, not so simple; I was never really good at this kind of thing, but will do my best to paint you the picture.

We attune ourselves to various signals of all kinds—high, low, positive, negative, strong, weak—whatever we're attracted to at the moment. And the mother of all signals, the main underlying current that feeds and sustains every conceivable combination of field outputs, is that of Divine Love. We live it every moment; how is it possible that anyone can dispute this?

The trick is to sort through all the noise, all the transient signals that aren't really useful or important—and yet which so easily distract us, even where I am—and locate and "match" the vibration of the one frequency that is making all of us possible.

How do I know this? Because I'm living proof of it. Your love and devotion, which has been sustaining and nurturing this body for so long in this state—didn't everyone tell you I'd be gone a long time ago?—is helping me to keep this sweet connection with you by matching the energy you so willingly give every moment.

Even if the body weren't here, you know I'd still be with you guys every day, right? <u>But</u>, because of your care, support, and love, we've been able to keep the amplification "up," at a level that confounds the medical community. It takes focus and intention—you're always saying this, Ma—to get the job done.

From my perspective, it seems that in America, the young people are focused on their bodies, all right, but aren't seeing beyond the surface. So much attention is paid to "how thin am I? . . . how good looking am I? . . . what kind of a fashion statement am I?" They're missing the point entirely, of course, because they're not seeing the whole picture. I talk to kids all the time about this over here—kids who have abused their systems in one way or another, passing up opportunities that will not come around again for a long time for them.

But this isn't confined just to the younger generations. EVERYBODY is responsible for understanding and <u>really getting</u> that we are much, much more than only a body, no matter what shape it is in. Having the opportunity to be in physical form, in whatever condition, is honestly a sacred trust and experience.

We all see it so much more clearly from here, of course. I guess what I'm trying to get across is that we don't have to make our lives so complicated—that wasn't the original intention, when we first achieved conscious awareness of ourselves. The whole point of amplification is to "echo" or repeat back, sound back, the core vibration—which emanates from all things around us, if only we tune in to the frequency. This isn't complicated or difficult; it's a matter of listening or attuning ourselves properly.

Just what does this really mean? It means, Ma and Pa, that we have to get rid of all the junk around us long enough to "hear" or absorb that one vibration. Okay, so how does that happen? All the great spiritual and now even scientific teachers or masters have given us lots of ways to "be still, and know that I am God." Meditations, chanting, breathing, singing (right, Ma?), praying, healing. There are loads of ways to take just a few minutes each day to "tune in."

I want to go back to that saying a few lines back. You can look at just those few simple words in multiple ways. Check it out:

Besides the traditional **"Be still and know that I am God,"** it can also be:

> **"Be still. And know that. I am God."**
> **"Be still and know that I am, God."**
> **"Be still, And know. That, I am. God."**
> **"Be still and know. That I am. God."**

All those years of Bible training have been paying off! I'm still amazed at how we all feel we just have to complicate things to make them work for us. I mean, to become inspired, we don't have to get all dressed up in fancy clothes and make a big deal out of meeting once a week (or month, or year) in a church. Inspiration is inherent in our core being; it's our very nature. It's who we really are, and even more important, it's <u>what</u> we are. Any time that we're either not inspired or inspiring, we're not being our true selves. How's <u>that</u> for something to chew on?!?

Okay, so what does this ultimately mean? Why is this even significant? Until we all really understand that our <u>one and only reason for being</u> is to amplify and transmit back the core signal or vibration/frequency/song—whatever you want to call it—we're just going to keep splitting, dividing, and repeating the same experiences over and over again until we figure out that all we have to

REALLY do is <u>send back</u> the signal we've been receiving for so long.

And each of us has a unique way, which we each have to discover for ourselves, of first listening to and locating the Divine Love frequency, absorbing it, and then amplifying it within ourselves sufficiently to a degree that we can then transmit it. Simple as that.

All this goes beyond and underneath a cellular level; it affects the very pattern of all life. As you've probably guessed by now, once one of us does this, and then more and more of us sustain that frequency emission, the pattern of our existence and our actuality will reflect in a way altogether more glorious than we can possible imagine. And to think that it all comes down to listening! Can you believe it?!?

Even here, we hear people say frequently, "Well, it's easy for you to say this and do this—but I just can't concentrate long enough. It doesn't work for me. I don't have time for that." You know what I'm talking about, Pa—the million and one excuses, right? Well, [I'm saying that] we don't have time for anything else but to start <u>now</u> with listening. I'm not a super religious kind of guy, but I do know that I believe in what I've experienced. And I can tell you that I've seen a lot of things, but this is the most important "thing" I've learned so far. We know we're all connected, in ways most of us can't even imagine—and wouldn't want to know. What one of us does, even for a small period of time, affects all of us—everywhere, in all of time and out of time.

I know, I know; I'm sounding "preachy" again. Well, I can't help it. For something that is so basic and fundamental to our very existence and to the existence of all livings things (and as most of us are missing the point entirely in our "lives"), we really have to make an effort to turn the tide now.

One of the kids I was talking with the other day said that this all reminded him of giving a laptop to a gorilla and expecting him to figure out how to use it, rather than bash it against some rocks. But, really, the concept is not that difficult to understand. When we really begin to "get" that creating this level of energy is what we're here for—and when we actually do it, the process increases exponentially on its own, by giving and receiving this frequency more and more. It's self-sustaining and regenerative.

Think about that. This is what the universe (you know, the "one verse"!) is all about. When we get all caught up with our own worries, anxieties, and individual ego problems, we are literally out of tune, or out of balance, with the universe. We spin out on a vibration of restriction and constriction, rather than one that is constantly expanding.

Everything, <u>every</u> thing, reduces to the one Divine Love frequency/tone/vibration. That means, Ma and Pa, every thought, every action, every word. We don't have to go around beating ourselves up for getting off track, or even off the road map; the universe is a very forgiving place. All we have to do is remind ourselves—frequently—to get back "in tune." As the saying goes, "practice makes perfect."

So, the next time someone comes up to you and says, "Gosh, I wish I had done such and such." Or, "I wish my life were going better." Or, "I regret I didn't get such and such done sooner"—just remind him or her that there's always <u>now</u> to get started. Every person here has at least one prime opportunity, and usually multiple opportunities— every single day—to tune in and listen, absorb, and reflect back this unique frequency. Gratitude and appreciation often jump-start the process. But somewhere, somehow—someone or something will come into your life and will provide the opportunity for you to "shine." This is what we all know here. Yes, we have to work at it, too, because our habits are pretty strongly ingrained. I love interacting with all the people I come into contact with—

it's enlightening _and_ inspiring!! And if anyone asks you, "How do you know when you're correctly tuning in at the right vibration?" Just tell them that they'll _know_ it when they _feel_ it. It's not an intellectual exercise, it's the _feeling_ of a "peace that passeth all understanding."

That's the closest I can come to describing how I've experienced it. It's like knowing that you're home again, that you've always been home, that you never left, and that you're waking up to remembering what you've always known. That's how it is with me and all of you, every day, every moment. I love you guys, always and in _all ways_. I am so proud to be with you!

With all my love,
—Jay

I have had to read this letter many times, as it contains so much spiritual information. When I have shared this letter with others, without exception, it seems to give people new insights into their own spirituality.

⁓

> *Believe that God resides in all beings;*
> *speak such words as will spread goodness,*
> *truth, and beauty; do such acts as will*
> *promote the happiness and prosperity of all;*
> *pray that all the worlds have peace. Expand*
> *yourselves; do not contract into your own*
> *tiny individuality. Expand into universal*
> *love, unshaken equanimity, and ever-active*
> *virtue. This is the path that will bring out the*
> *divinity in you to the fullest.*
>
> —Sri Sathya Sai Baba[39]

---

39 *Sathya Sai Speaks* 12:16, April 1973

CHAPTER 13

"SHARE THE LETTERS!"

After 2007's wonderful "New Year's" communication, that year brought us more challenges, including physical pain. This time it was my pain, which finally ended after my having back surgery in August 2007. On July 7 ("7-7-07," an auspicious date), I woke up with excruciating pain in my back and left hip. It seemed that many people we knew were going through physical pain and what we called "tough karma." We had dealt with Ron's valleys in pain, and Jay at this time had been in his condition for thirteen years.

Now it was my turn—talk about feeling like "running a marathon in mud"! I was more physically disabled than I have ever been in my life. I literally couldn't walk or stand for long. The doctors thought the source of the pain was a slipped disc, but the real source was not discovered until during surgery, when a cyst was found on the spinal column, pressing on the nerve tissue. The cyst was removed, and the surgery did bring relief, though I had to walk with a cane for many months afterward.

The following year, in July 2008, I traveled again to India for a World Education Conference held at Prasanthi Nilayam, Sai Baba's ashram. I had been invited to be a speaker on the last day of the conference, during a plenary session that took place during morning darshan. Phyllis Krystal, a good friend who used to live in California and now lives in Zurich, Switzerland, was also scheduled to speak, along with two young ladies, one from Argentina and the other from India. But, to our surprise, as we were getting ready to speak and had been called up front to "the veranda,"[40] Baba went into the interview room and called just us ladies in for an interview—instead of having us speak.

It had been over eleven years since I had been privileged to talk with Baba on a personal level, and I was very happy to have this opportunity. Of course, this surprise interview session was a little troubling for the conference organizers, because now their morning schedule had been disrupted, and Baba was in the interview room, talking to the expected speakers for the morning.

While the audience waited, the college boys started leading *bhajans* (devotional songs), and

---

40 The veranda of the original devotional hall or *mandir*, built around 1950, now forms the dais for the current, immense, open-sided darshan hall, which was added on in the early 1990s.

they sang for an hour—with the singers' voices and the sounds of their instruments being broadcast at high volume over the loudspeakers—while we were in the interview room talking with Baba. I liked what Phyllis called our encounter—a "tea party" with the Lord. And that was what it was like—very personal and sweet, with just us ladies and Mother Sai. He allowed me to come up close so he could speak with me more privately. Because of the loud music and Baba's very soft voice, I had to put my hands on the arms of his wheelchair and bend my ear very close to his mouth so I could hear him.

He reminded me that I had a good husband and that I should not argue with him. This is a topic Baba has discussed with me on several other occasions. I think he does this quite often with married couples, and I'm sure most of us do have our times of disagreements. I said to him, "I just don't understand him (my husband) at times!"

He replied to me so sweetly, "It's not *understand*, it's *misunderstand*."

Of course, he was right. Most of the arguments we have are simply misunderstandings, and many times we are saying the same thing, but coming from a different angle, thereby producing the misunderstanding.

Baba made all of us *vibhuti* to eat. It was so fine and white in color, and the aroma was wonderful. Then he materialized *vibhuti* for Phyllis and me to take home with us. I watched closely as he placed his hand over my hand. Rubbing his thumb, index finger, and middle finger together, he materialized a pile of *vibhuti*, which streamed downward into the palm of my hand. Then he gave us pieces of paper, in which to wrap the precious ash so we could take it home with us.

I had trouble folding my paper, and Baba asked me to hand it to him, so he could show me how to wrap it properly. We laughed; he took the paper and ever so gently wrapped it, then handed it back to me. Our hands were still covered with *vibhuti*, so he took his handkerchief and rubbed away the excess on my hands, just like a mother would clean her child's hands after eating something.

Baba was very sweet with all of us. He talked to the two single girls about marriage and said he would send them husbands. He made Phyllis's granddaughter a gold chain with a gold pendant and put it around her neck. She was very happy. He hit me on the head and commanded me, "Be happy!"

I told him I still had bouts of depression at times, and he told me to pray when I feel this way. Then, looking at me with so much compassion and love in his eyes, he said, *I'm always with you; I'm above you, around you, and inside you, don't worry.* His words were so loving that I broke into tears. And

I knew from many personal experiences that this was absolutely the truth. I have remembered those words time and again. They not only give me confidence in times of uncertainty, they also return to my mind whenever things happen that demonstrate Baba's omniscience and omnipresence.

In that interview, I had a chance to ask about Jay's letters. Sharing them always seemed to bring a positive response, and people would tell me, "Berniece, you must write a book and put these letters in it." I needed to have confirmation that it would be all right to share these letters, so I asked Baba about the letters and whether I should share them.

He told me, "Share." Then again, before the interview was over, he instructed me twice more to "share the letters."

When I returned home after this trip, I contacted Debbie again and told her of my encounter with Baba, and that he had told me to share the letters. I needed her permission, too, to publish the letters. She was very happy about it. As she was dealing with some very serious health problems, I sent her some *vibhuti* and lingam water.

Shortly thereafter, during a quiet time on a Monday in late August, Debbie reconnected with Jay's vibration. This time he did not address his communication as a letter; he just started in with the message, and ended without a sign-off.

In his previous letter, Jay had talked about vibration and frequencies. In this letter, he continued to develop the theme of interpreting life as energy frequencies and vibrations, and that science and spirituality will eventually merge.

He mentions peering "through this glass darkly," describing what it is like for the coma patient to function in two worlds at once. Interestingly, over ten years earlier, at the end of 1997, one of the most vivid art pieces that Jay had "painted" for us, through Debbie, he had called "Coma: Through the World Darkly." (See page 163.)

LETTER 11

Monday, August 25, 2008, 11:44 p.m.

When you are **all-one** with every-thing around you, how can you possibly be **a-lone**? Change your perception or **view**-point."

Of course, we're busy (those of us in comas, with a foot in both worlds simultaneously). It takes tremendous will power and great reserves of energy to peer through this glass darkly. Only with unending support from loving beings around us are we able to perform our duties in the physical and nonphysical "realities." Talk about having a "split personality" (just joking).

Be grateful to and for the amazing vehicles each of us resides within. These are the top-of-the-line, incredible, "tricked out" models that are the ultimate bio-organic answers to the concepts of recycle, reduce, reuse, and repair. Just think about it—where else can you ride around in a first-rate vehicle that sustains itself for as long as a body does? Do we take the time to talk to our millions of cells, thanking them for the dedicated, hard work they perform 24/7? And how often do we listen to them?

From a little bit different perspective, all of life is comprised of energy responding to or reacting with itself. Energy frequencies, "power surges," and vibrations are represented in various ways. One of those ways is the manifesting of, and through, physical form.

Our perception is how we interpret the vibration that we think is separate from ourselves. You'll probably have to read THAT one again. (Ha, ha.) It all seems **so real**. And it is, to a certain degree, but not necessarily in the way we translate what we experience by use of our physical senses.

(An aside: Ma/Pa, do you want to know why Sai Baba insists that men and women sit separately? It's not so much for a moral reason—although that is involved. It's because the energy patterns of a man are vastly different than those of a woman. When the two are together or even near each other, the amount of energy generated by the adjacent, differing patterns literally "distracts" the "individuals" from focusing on the higher energy before them—God. Separation of the genders helps to cut down on the amount of "interference" and "static" in the group. This makes even more sense when you can actually see it in action.)

A personal example is how I am perceived in my physical form. From all outward appearances, it looks like I'm mostly not here, unable to respond well enough to communicate effectively, physically, what I am experiencing. I can hear just fine. And, believe it or not, I have moments when I can see pretty darn well, too. Not much for talking, though—not _yet_, anyway. My other senses are very highly tuned—sense of touch, intonation, noise levels, emotions of those around me. Believe me, there's a whole lot more going on inside me than you can imagine! And what is sustaining this "Cadillac" of a vehicle I'm riding in? The highest and most valuable pure energy in existence, of existence—love. All of the kindness and love of those around me, inside and out, allows this body to continue operating. And love communicates across _all_ barriers and levels of existence, because its very nature is to expand and permeate through every square inch of life in all forms. Love is life in all forms, right down to the tiniest product of be-ingness. And this is how science and spirituality will eventually merge—through the understanding and demonstration that the infinite energy of un-conditional love IS everything, in various contexts. The next step up from that, is acknowledging that each of us _is_ that love, and we are indeed _all one_.

As human beings in this earthly realm, we carry the temporary entry ticket to all kinds of rides in this amusement park. Some rides are thrilling, some are scary, and many are downright entertaining. And what do we want to do when taking these "rides?" We want **to share** them with others. (Right, Ma? Couldn't resist this!) I mean, how often do you see rides with only one seat, right??? The laughter, the tears, the thrills, the fears—all of these are for us to experience and relate with others. Why? So that we <u>practice</u> communicating as one energy to another, ultimately to integrate ourselves with all that is. How obvious!

Just as each one of our cells communicates with everything around it—passing on energy and in-formation, recharging, repairing, and recycling—so, too, do we, on all of our awareness levels, act the same. Our emotional states are reflected in our physical states; energy creates patterns constantly. It's very important to see why denser energy states of emotion such as anger, resentment, and frustration affect the body as well, due to the broadcasting ef-fect on all of the organs and cellular structures. Soft, gentle, quiet, and calm states are much more ben-eficial and conducive for expanding and sustaining the higher states of appreciation, compassion, and love—for oneself and everything around us.

In the message above, Jay made a humorous reference to "sharing" being a natural inclination we all have. I believe he was underscoring not only the fact that I wanted quite naturally to share his letters with others but also the fact that Sai Baba had emphasized to me to "share."

> *Self-imposed discipline is conducive to real peace—peace of mind, poise, equanimity, and the stable equilibrium of the mind. Peace of mind is the most desirable thing in this world. It gives us physical and psychic euphoria. In order to achieve this peace, an aspirant must develop a thirst for spiritual wisdom. He must also acquire the qualities of love, sympathy, and compassion, and do selfless service to others. Peace should not be regarded as a part-time virtue to be cultivated only during meditation. It is a constant state of inner tranquility. It should become habitual and instinctive.*
>
> —Sri Sathya Sai Baba[41]

---

41 *Summer Showers in Brindavan 1979*, ch. 17, p. 128.

The next day, as Debbie waited in her car in front of her daughter's high school, Jay came to her again. She spoke to him, and Jay had a few words to say to her about nature and the beauty around her, almost as if picking right up from his last discussion about communicating with "all that is" and getting into a state of appreciation. Here he gives us insight into the "etheric" corollaries of the physical senses—amazing visual and auditory impressions—through his description of the beauty, colors, and vibrant "living" energy of nature.

On a humorous note, he starts in by greeting Debbie with "*Buenos*"—an informal Spanish *hello*. (The word means "good"—short for *buenos días* or "good day.") Most of the nurses' aides (CNAs) at Jay's facility are of Hispanic descent, and they speak Spanish around him all the time. It appears he's picking up on some of the Spanish phrases.

LETTER 12

Tuesday, August 26, 2008, 12:40 p.m. (waiting for Debbie's daughter, Katie, in front of her high school, to take her to a medical appointment)

Good afternoon, Jay.

Buenos, Debbie! New greeting—you like it? (Jay is smiling.) I'm practicing some Spanish because many of the people I work with at the moment like to use that language.

Have you ever thought about color? Look around you. Take a good, long look—slowly.

(Debbie's note: The view is of a large lawn in front of the school; trees are beginning to turn to fall colors of orange and gold.)

This is the <u>living</u> landscape. And yet what you perceive is but a fraction of what is truly "real." From where I am, I see the <u>vibration</u> of the landscape: the turning leaves on the trees are shimmering, glowing, emanating waves of vitality and essence. Actually, they look like they're showing off! (Ha, ha!) And why not? As they ready for yet another transformation in their own life cycle, they are showing and telling us of the resplendence and glory of life itself. Before shriveling up and falling to the ground with the "appearance" of lifelessness, they provide a dazzling display of beingness.

The same goes for the green grass. It is sparkling, vibrant, and vital in this late summer sun. The blades of grass blowing in the breeze have the sound of miniature glass slivers tinkling against each other. The lawn before you is at the peak of this part of its life cycle, before appearing "dormant" in winter, when it will look dull. And yet, this life energy is never dormant; it is simply in a process of constant expression. And it is just as we are—in a perpetually moving process of transformation and expression.

About a week later, in the first week of September 2008, Jay and Debbie "met" again, and the following letter came through. Once again, Jay seemed to pick up right where he had left off the week before when talking about energy and living things, and about how everything affects everything else . . . living things and their parts, emotions, energy, awareness.

LETTER 13

Tuesday, September 2, 2008, 10:26 p.m.

D: Hi Jay, late evening seems to work better for me at the moment. Okay with you?

J: Hey, Debbie! Thanks for meeting with me and taking down notes on everything. I know you're not at your physical best, but when did *that* ever stop either one of us?!? Ha!! Use a pen—that's better—easier on the hand movement.

(Note from Debbie: I had been using a pencil.)

I can see the maelstrom you're in at this time

(Note from Debbie: I was recovering from the most recent surgery, having to get back in the job market, find medical insurance—it was overwhelming at times.)

<u>Don't</u> <u>worry</u>. You know, we often put so much energy into fussing and fuming over a problem or situation, that we actually prevent or postpone the solution from happening. How's that for a double bind?! The solution is right here for you—yes, within sight, and it will ease your mind to let it unfold <u>naturally</u>. So, stop worrying; start moving in a forward

direction. You <u>are</u> heading in the right direction; the wheels are in motion, and things will be chugging along very soon—in a <u>positive</u> <u>way</u>. Have faith. And keep on "clearing"—mentally, physically, emotionally, and spiritually.

D: Thanks, Jay! I feel better already! What message(s) or ideas would you like to tell the folks? You know, your mom is writing a book about all this, and she got Sai Baba's blessing to <u>share</u> your letters! In an interview, no less!

J: Well, it's <u>about</u> <u>time</u>, Ma! (Ha, ha.) Just *who* do you think has been buggin' him about giving you the message to get going on this material??? He'd wave me down, saying, "Soon, soooon. Be patient."

I'm really glad you're getting this down in print, Ma. I know it's a lot of work, but it's <u>good</u> work, and it's time to get this done. I mean, heck, you've got other books in line after this one! (laughing)

Remember, Ma and Pa (I <u>love</u> calling you guys that!), how we talked about energy and cells in the body? Well, even Sai Baba talks about all of us being cells in the body of the One, like notes in a song. We all have jobs to do, work to do, roles to play. (Yes, I'm attuned to your thoughts and conversations about this). When we're "on target" or "hitting our mark," we're in the flow, right? We're doing the work we're assigned to do and communicating well with those around us (most of the time), to keep the system running smoothly, consistently.

But what happens when we deviate from our given tasks and become distracted, or diseased? The area in which we operate can begin to malfunction, and we go off into a ditch. This happens a lot through emotional or physical trauma, and poor mental habits. Those around us then have to work even harder to maintain balance, equilibrium, and functionality. In other words, adaptability, flexibility, patience, tolerance, and selfless service all contribute to healing the dis-eased individual, so that he/she can resume functioning as part of a team in a positive, productive way. This doesn't mean that things always will return to the way they used to be; in fact, in order to expand, grow, learn, and experience, we must welcome our "challenges" as blessings in disguise.

This letter, which like the previous two ended rather abruptly, started out with some encouragement for Debbie. She had been applying for jobs just as the job market appeared to be drying up. And as Jay suggested, things did resolve for her over the next few months, unfolding in a very supportive and positive way.

The next day, Jay had more to communicate about energy and its relationship in our bodies. Building on his association in his career with amusement parks that have thrill rides, he continued to develop this analogy to bring out more spiritual lessons.

LETTER 14

Wednesday, September 3, 2008, 7:51 p.m.

I want to return to the amusement park analogy because it's one I personally relate to. People come from all over to experience "the thrill of a lifetime." It's exactly the same for us, as souls riding around in these temporary, hi-tech vehicles. We come for "the thrill of a lifetime." It's a brief time when we can have all kinds of opportunities to experience life in various modes/rides.

But when the theme park closes, people go home, right? They are usually excited, exhausted, and thoroughly over-stimulated by their day's experiences. And although some of the rides seemed or looked dangerous—in reality, they are very well-regulated, and maintained by personnel behind the scenes. Hidden cameras allow special staff to watch each ride meticulously.

The same is true of our souls in these earthly bodies. Yes, "mishaps" occur occasionally, as with my situation, but these are <u>not</u> accidents. Really. It's all part of the "show." Just because our vehicles (bodies) sustain damage or wear out with age does not mean that the driver (soul) is harmed in any way. Ma, Pa, how else would you know—<u>really</u>

<u>get</u> <u>it</u>—that we continue on, no matter how strong or convincing the physical illusion may seem?

Obviously, I am still here. I haven't gone anywhere. I'm not lost, alone (far from it!), or "stuck" anywhere. I'm busier now than ever. Pretty soon, everyone will be able to communicate with whomever they want, in whatever state of consciousness they happen to be—just like the invention of the telephone, only better. And it will seem so natural.

All of the "minimally functioning" people you guys see in the physical realm are actually very active, productive individuals whom I can see and work with from where I am. We know what our jobs are; we choose those positions we feel most suited for, and we <u>still</u> manage to be connected to the physical body. Tiring? You cannot imagine! And yet, I can say without hesitation that I am happy to be doing this work—it's <u>cutting edge!!</u>

I wish I could simply open my eyes normally and tell you both all this myself. One day soon, you will see me regain consciousness for a brief time and communicate directly with you, but only for a very short time. Just to let you know. Even more important, you <u>do</u> know that we've always been together, through thick 'n' thin.

The world is not what you think it is or how you see it. It really is more akin to a theme park. We all have our jobs. You can tell we're making progress when we've "graduated" from <u>being entertained</u> to <u>providing the entertainment</u>! The next step up is to work behind the scenes—assisting, facilitating, and ensuring that all the rides operate accordingly. All the scenes are set. The show must and will go on, right? It does so—flawlessly. And we <u>all</u> follow the guidance from the Director. (smiling)

Now, I'd like to ask a favor of you both. I was wondering if you could pick out a book, something easy and entertaining, like an old Hardy Boys mystery, something along those lines. And what I'd like to try out is having you read it, slowly, to me, for about ten to fifteen minutes at a time, to start. I want to see if I can sharpen up my focusing abilities better, so I don't drift in and out as much. The reason I'm asking for a simple book to start with, is that the language has to be simple. Know what I mean? Anyway, let's give it a try and see what happens. I'm rewiring parts of the brain and need to see if certain circuits will light up or not. Wasn't planning on being an electrician! (Ha, ha!)

 Okay, that's it for now. I've got to get back to some other things that need taking care of. And I'd better not wear out my writing partner here. (grinning)

One more thing. You know, we always wonder if we are strong enough, good enough, brave enough to handle what life throws at us. The answer is: <u>yes, we are</u>. We always have been and always will be. No doubt about it!

I love you both with all my heart (and it's a BIG heart!)

—Jay

In this letter, Jay made some amazing statements. He seemed to be giving a prediction that the "veil" or gap of communication between the physical and etheric realms is going to get a lot easier to bridge, or perhaps even between humans, despite various kinds of "distances." He also talked about his regaining consciousness for a brief time—a thrilling idea but one we try not to get too excited about or attached to. Regardless, it is clear from this letter that he is working very hard internally with the physical body, to "reconnect the circuits."

After we received this letter, we did begin to read some of "The Hardy Boys" to Jay, and still do on occasion, but not every day.

༺༻

If (circumstances) harm the body, sages are unaffected, because they know that they are not the body! As to harming the soul, sages know that this is impossible, for the soul is ever in bliss! By means of sadhana *(spiritual discipline, practice), become that type of sage, unaffected by pleasure and pain, loss or gain, victory or defeat.*

—Sri Sathya Sai Baba[42]

---

42 *Sathya Sai Speaks* 17:17, quote at end of discourse.

CHAPTER 14

WITH GREAT LOVE

Everyone should act according to the motto, "Help ever, hurt never." . . . The Lord is described as the Indweller of the heart, so love and compassion are inherent in every person. Each has to share this love with others. Failure to share one's love is gross ingratitude to society, to which one owes everything. One should give one's love freely to others and receive love in return. This is the deep significance of human life.

—Sri Sathya Sai Baba[43]

43 *Sathya Sai Speaks,* 27:16, June 4, 1994.

We received another letter from Jay the following month, on October 18, 2008; at first, this one was somewhat heart-wrenching for us, because he talked about what it had been like for him in the beginning, right after his transitional experience. He had never shared this much detail with us, or about his initial disorientation. We had never considered the distress he might have been experiencing at that time, and it was painful to imagine what it was like, from his descriptions. Yet what he shared with us also gave us insight into the rescue work that Jay has been involved in since this event and increased our awareness of what happens to people after they "cross over" or enter a coma or transition state suddenly. Jay describes an "etheric" world that sounds as full of form, color, activity, beings (including animals), and function, as our physical world.

At this time, in the fall of 2008, the world financial picture looked like it was coming apart at the seams. The economy was in a huge crisis, with people losing their homes, jobs, and savings, and a great deal of uncertainty, if not panic and anger, in many people's minds. In this letter, Jay refers again, indirectly, to his ability to hear very well—referring to the broadcast news, which he can hear, obviously, when the TV in his room is on.

He touches on the economic times—which have been difficult for very many people—and he offers up some advice for us all, that *helping each other* to alleviate our fears and anxieties is "where it's at"—the real solution in terms of the vibration we broadcast and how we influence each other—in periods of crisis. He had ended some of his previous letters with *Love*, or *Love, love, love*; this letter he closes, *With Great Love, Jay.*

LETTER 15

Dear Ma and Pa,

So glad to be writing to you again! You know, it may not seem like it, but those of us in these "semi-conscious" (actually, hyper-conscious) states are completely aware of what's happening in the "outside" world. Heck, we can <u>hear it</u> blaring on the news, and our senses are very highly attuned to the energies all around us. Not only do we hear/sense the news from televisions, we also hear everyone talking about the mess our world is in right now. The fear lingers in the air like a cold fog.

I want to tell you a story. When I first found myself in this state of being—sometimes here, sometimes there, who knows where—I felt lost, confused, and unsure of where to turn for help. I mean, it was difficult for me, on *all* levels, to maneuver. I didn't exactly "see" clearly; things and people appeared blurry, out of focus, and fuzzy. I couldn't move in the body, but I could hear okay. I couldn't see clearly, and I felt like I was wandering in a dark space and place most of the time—like groping in the dark for a light switch. I started to panic a little and began to move faster—which only made me stumble over myself and lose my balance. I was starting to feel afraid, all alone, in a kind of dark maze or labyrinth. And you know what I did? I thought of you both and Jan, and that calmed me down.

Then, I wondered what you would do if you were in my shoes. And I sat down and heard you, Ma, say to me, "Pray for help, Jay; pray for help." My praying up to then was kind of rusty, if you know what I mean. (Jay laughing.) But I could hear your voice as clear as day, Ma, and that's just what I did. I sat quietly, got myself together, and prayed to every angel and Jesus for help. I even prayed to Sai Baba for help, Ma and Pa, because I figured he'd know who I was, right?? (Ha, ha!)

Well, it worked! In the far distance, I saw a small dot of light that got bigger and bigger, coming toward me, until everything was a brilliant, shining light. Two people were in that light—a man and a woman. They looked like ordinary people, just like you and me, and they appeared because I had asked for help. They didn't have wings or halos, or anything like that—I had sort of expected some kind of angel to appear to fly me away to a promised land! They wore jeans, shirts, shoes—pretty ordinary-looking, except that they had this amazing light radiating from them.

This wasn't the only time I received help in the beginning; I've had <u>many</u> times of finding myself in the dark, asking for help. It takes practice to finally "get" the idea that we are fully capable of radiating our own light! What distinguished this particular episode is that these two people explained to me what was happening to me, with me. Like me, they were also "half here and half there," meaning that they were not dead. In fact, they were both very much alive and still embodied in the earth realm. And it is they (along with others like me) who helped me adapt and adjust to being in the physical world as well as being in a much broader, etheric world.

It took <u>time</u> to make this adjustment—and a lot of work! Now, I am in the position to help others (usually younger teenagers) to adapt and adjust to similar circumstances, to work with their bodies, and to communicate with those around them on both levels. The more awareness we have of ourselves, the more light we bring to those around us. This holds true on every level of existence.

So, why am I talking about this? Because so many people of all ages in the world today are experiencing fear and panic over all kinds of things: money, the stock market, jobs, retirement, failures of one kind or another, wars, housing, oil, the end of the world. We hear this all the time, but the <u>volume of intensity</u> has risen sharply in the past couple of months, and especially in the last few weeks.

And what is <u>really</u> happening? Circumstances in the world have changed enough so that people don't recognize where they are or who they are. They find themselves backed into a dark and scary corner that is unfamiliar. They can't see clearly, and they feel as if they are losing their balance, stumbling, looking for answers, for some light to be shed on their situation.

Please tell them, Ma, that all they have to do is to sit still, in the quiet, and ask for help. Pray for guidance. And wait patiently. Help will come, I am one hundred percent sure of that. I am living proof of it!

And do you know what the real solution—the real key—is, to this worldwide panic and fear?? It's so simple that most people overlook it at first, until it settles in one's mind and heart. The answer to all of this is to <u>help each other</u>. Find out what someone else's needs are—and help them. It doesn't mean you have to support them, just do one thing every day to help someone in need. Help can be as simple as opening a door for someone, extending a helping hand, or giving a friendly greeting to someone you don't know. Just one thing a day, given with love and compassion, to a "stranger," is all that is needed to turn the fear into peace.

In order for us to really understand that we are interconnected to such a degree that we **are** each other, we first have to take small steps toward reconnecting with each other. And this is done by sharing. You will be guided by both seen and unseen forces to develop your amazing potential of sharing "goodness and prosperity" with others—to lighten their (and your) burdens.

So many people worry about and think that money is the answer. But money is a byproduct of a much larger "fortune" residing within all of us. Yes, money is necessary to live in this world, but it is not representative of our inherent birthright, which is to be human, in the highest sense of those words. To be human—human beings—we must demonstrate and radiate who and what we really are: compassionate, loving, balanced be-ings, here to help and support others so that our combined energy, or radiance, provides the light needed to see ourselves and the world clearly—with focus, with vision, and with appreciation. No matter what the external world seems like, it is our duty and responsibility to share (get it, Ma? Ha, ha—I couldn't resist!) the light from within us, to all those in need.

So, if you find yourself in a state of worry or anxiety, or if you feel you're in the dark, stop! Sit still. Collect yourself. And then ask for help. You have no idea how thin the veil is between this physical world of illusion and other worlds. It is transparent, almost. There are an infinite number of people who can and will assist you in whatever situation you find yourself. I might be one of them! (Jay smiling)

Just pay it forward, as the saying goes. As you receive help, pass it on, in whatever way you can. Then, you will see the world around you with clearer vision. It's not what you think it is! There is *so much more* waiting for you to explore and discover. Let's ALL participate in the adventure of a lifetime!

I love you all so much, and I appreciate everything you're doing for and with me! Love the stories—keep 'em coming!

With great love,
—Jay

In the letter above, Jay again brought up a little humor about "sharing," while pointing up its importance. This hit home for me, because, despite Sai Baba's direct command to me to "share," when I had asked him about sharing Jay's letters, I still had recurring doubts. Sometimes, when I would talk to people about the idea, they would react negatively, so at times I would become discouraged and stuck. This was all part of my lessons in maintaining equanimity and, as Sai Baba talks about, keeping a steady mind in the face of either praise or blame. I think Jay was trying to cheer me up and cheer me on in the book project, using it as an example of the principle he was trying to convey.

He also counsels us all to use prayer to ask for help—to pray for guidance, and it will come. His message in this letter was a powerful and inspiring statement of how to use our faith and know that divine help is ours for the asking, and that by sharing and helping others we fulfill our purpose in "being human."

༄

God proclaimed: **Ask and it shall be given; seek and you will find; knock and the door will be opened.**

You are not asking the right source.
You are asking the world and not God, the
Creator of the world. How can you get a
response? You are also not searching for
the right thing. You are searching only for
wealth and position, which are unworthy and
transient. At what door are you knocking?
The door of grief! (Then,) how can you
get ananda *(bliss)? If you comply with the*
directions of the Divine correctly, you will
get appropriate results. If you open the door
of your heart and love God, you get what
you need. Do not ask for any petty boon. Ask
for God Himself. He can give you anything
and everything you need. Pray for the love of
God; you will get love. Through divine love
you will have prosperity here and hereafter.

—Sri Sathya Sai Baba[44]

44 *Sathya Sai Speaks* 31:14, Apr. 20, 1998.

CHAPTER 15

HAPPY NEW YEAR, 2009

Happiness and sorrow have to be experienced in worldly life, as they are as inevitable as the sunset and sunrise. You think the New Year will give better experiences, but this is not correct. It is the mind that is responsible for pleasure and pain. If your mind is good, you will find everything good. Without God's grace, living itself would be impossible. Even the troubles you may experience are gifts of the Divine. You are embodiments of the Divine, which is nothing but bliss. While being so, is it not folly on your part to say that you are suffering from pain and grieve over it?

—Sri Sathya Sai Baba[45]

45 *Sathya Sai Speaks* 27:1, Jan. 1, 1994.

We were quite surprised to receive yet another letter from Jay, just a few months later, on New Year's Day, 2009. As usual, his communication was greatly appreciated by us and filled with many spiritual truths; Jay calling us *Ma* and *Pa* always warmed our hearts and brought back a lot of happy memories. It reminded me of the times we would sit at the kitchen table, sometimes being silly and other times having serious talks about truths and things in general.

In this letter, he also mentions some congestion he was having; his physical body had been sick at the time he communicated this letter to Debbie. Debbie, of course, being hundreds of miles away and not in regular contact with us, did not know that Jay was sick, so this was yet another confirmation that he slipped into the letter's contents.

Also, he talks about the ongoing lessons that he is learning in the spiritual realm. It appears that whether in a body or outside one, our lessons just keep on unfolding. And again he addresses the heavy concerns of "the world"—which was in the throes of a recession and financial failures—and how *all* are experiences for our good.

LETTER 16

January 1, 2009, 6:12 p.m. – 7:27 p.m.
Santa Rosa, CA

Dear Ma and Pa and Jan,

Here it is, a brand new year, 2009 by your calendar. Many happy greetings and my infinite gratitude and love to you both for being here with me, for me, and for never giving up on me. I know I still look pretty "vacant" at times, but underneath my calm exterior lies a hotbed of activity and motion. What a paradox, and also what a wonder to know that the two kinds of *being* are completely dependent upon each other for continued survival in this earthly realm.

I've been deliberately staying cool where the channeling goes with Debbie, because I could see she needed the time and space to deal with the radiation treatments. Just to let you know, *I* was the one who had to cool it, because *she* kept trying to set up the communication. And once we both get going, it's hard to shut either one of us up! (Ha, ha!) This time, though, I put the brakes on, because it just would have delayed our communication even more if I had given in. So, I told her that if she waited, we'd send a letter to you today.

Yeah, I can be in control when I have to and when it's necessary. How the heck do you think I've been able to stay so long in my own physical body? This is more for her than for you. It's very important to follow the body's signals and needs, when the chips are down.

Have you ever given thought to what it means when someone says "Happy New Year?" That phrase contains many implied messages, and I have to tell you that from where I sit these days, those messages are kind of confusing for people living from one day to the next, year after year. In the reality I live in, time isn't really seen in the same way—or at all, for that matter. We don't measure ourselves by minutes, hours, days, weeks, months, or years. We expand our perspectives—by the kinds of experiences we have and are able to process thoroughly through our states of consciousness.

We don't always "get it right the first time" here, either. We act according to what we're presented with (and also by what we attract to ourselves); we experience the situation as deeply as we can and then take the time to review the outcome. Nothing is "good" or "bad," "positive" or "negative." Everything simply is. Everything is already in balance, no matter how we interpret it, react to it, or engage with it. Nothing needs to be fixed, changed, or improved upon. The experiences we choose to have and attract to ourselves are for our benefit, for our understanding, and ultimately for our growth.

That doesn't mean that I don't get frustrated or annoyed when it seems that I haven't handled a situation well—I still say some choice phrases when I see that I've goofed up! What happens is that this exact kind of experience will show up again and again, in all kinds of variations, until I "get" what I'm supposed to do. There's nothing sweeter than the realization that after so many times, I finally understand the meaning of the experience!

Okay, so you're wondering, "What does this have to do with 'Happy New Year'?"

While many may have the intention of wishing for others a happy year, or a new beginning, the idea is that one is relieved that the old year is finished (and good riddance to it), and/or the new year may be just as difficult as (if not more than) the previous one.

The other point I would like to make is the idea of *hoping* or *wishing* someone a happy, new year— that is, to project into the near future the elements of happiness. Especially at this time in our human development, the present and the immediate future hold several areas of great concern. We hear about this all the time. I'm wondering, Ma and Pa, how many of us really get that _all_ of our experiences are designed for our own highest good? It's so obvious to us, here where I am, to see that each and every moment that we're consciously awake and aware, we are benefiting from the momentary gifts of experience that are brought our way. Nothing is good or bad; everything is as it needs to be, <u>for our benefit</u>.

Knowing this helps us to accept everything that comes into our respective "orbits" as gifts—even, and <u>especially</u>, those things that frighten us or cause emotional reactions. It's human nature to react first, respond later. But a lot of us get stuck in a loop of reaction without even getting to the response phase. You know, there's a whole LOT of reaction going on in the world right now, and groups are stuck in that never-ending cycle of action/reaction, action/reaction, action/reaction. The same pattern repeats over and over, and we don't grow beyond the habit of constantly "firing."

But, just say that during one of those cycles, we somehow respond differently, sit back for a moment and simply look at what's happening. We just might <u>respond</u> in a way that breaks our habitual cycle of reaction, and as a result, the outcome ends up something surprising and wonderful. We neither stubbornly deny the experience nor cling to it with a desired, perpetual, hoped-for ending; we transcend our expectations/hopes/wishes and take the leap of faith required to grow beyond our expectations. We give ourselves permission to experience something beyond our recognition. Now *that's* what grace is all about!

So where does God fit into all of this? God is the force of unconditional love generating all of these experiences, generating all of us, creating the circumstances in which we have the opportunity to wake up. The questions we have to ask ourselves are: *Where are we right now? What are we doing/thinking/experiencing? Are we at peace with ourselves? Are we happy with this moment? And ultimately— are we grateful for each moment that provides us with yet another opportunity to "see more clearly"?*

Each day is a blessing; you say this yourself, Ma. I know, because I'm listening! (Ha, ha!)

Happy New Year? Most definitely! Even more to the point, Ma and Pa, happy new moment, happy for being here, happy to be with you both, and happy for all the opportunities in which I am able to experience life in all its glory. Happy to be alive!

We don't have to dwell on what was or what might have been; let's just be our best selves *now*, to the greatest extent possible. This is the best time to be alive, Ma and Pa, and Jan. We are all having tremendous experiences that are helping each of us to be much more than we think we are. Life has a wonderful way of showing us all that the universe is much more vast and miraculous than our minds can ever conceive of. So, let's not limit ourselves to worrying or being concerned with the future, because this time <u>now</u> is the most important moment of our lives. <u>Right now!</u> It always has been, and it will continue on for all time. How's <u>that</u> for cosmic vision?!? (Jay smiling).

 I've said it before and I'll say it again—you are the best family a guy could ever hope for! I am forever grateful for all of you, for your thoughts, your prayers, and especially your energy and devotion. I have a little congestion at the moment, but that should clear up soon. It doesn't stop me from sharing your "divine" healing!!

Remember that I love you a whole lot—always have, always will. Be happy!

> Love, from your "cosmic son" (ha ha!),
> —Jay

Jay reminds us, and I believe God is reminding us through Jay, to wake up from our slumber. He hints at the mystery and grandeur of embracing each experience that comes our way. It's time we realized who we really are and live to that potential. Can we not as human beings love one another as Jesus told us to do long ago? We MUST do that. It's time! It's time!

༄

> *The Upanishads say, "Get up, arise, awake!" Time is fleeing fast. Use the moment, while it is available, for the best of uses: the awareness of the Divine in all. When you die, you must die not like a tree or beast or worm, but like one who has realized that he is God. That is the consummation of all the years you spend in the human frame.*
>
> *—Sri Sathya Sai Baba*[46]

---

46 *Sathya Sai Speaks* 5:14, Mar. 25, 1965.

AFTERWORD
COMA : CO-OPERATIVE MUTUAL ASSISTANCE

By summer of 2009, I had completed a rough draft of this book, and after Debbie took a look at it, she took some time to contact Jay again. In this final letter, Jay shares more on the heightened sensory awareness of a coma patient, even when the eyes are closed.

Jay signs this letter as "Jay (boy)." I asked Debbie how she came to write this exact phrase, and she said, "I just write what I hear, but I wasn't sure about the word *boy*, so I put it in parentheses."

Jay had never used that particular expression before with Debbie, but for us it was very meaningful, because Jay used to call himself "Jay-boy." He would call me up on the phone and say, "Hello, Mammy! This here's Jay-boy!" It's little messages like these that help us truly feel—just as Jay is always telling us—that he is "right here" and "hasn't gone anywhere."

LETTER 17

Monday, July 27, 2009, 2:11 p.m. – 4:35 p.m.
(Debbie's note:)

Dear Jay,

I just finished reading your mom's book—it's amazing! And even though we've worked together for years now, the information and examples you give seem so new, or at least different, to me. I was wondering if you could and would elaborate more on your side of activity, what things are like for you now, how we can help other coma patients. And, of course, what do you think of your mom's book—anything to add?

Dear Ma and Pa,

I knew you could do it, Ma!! You will still be revising some here, editing some there, but you have captured the essence of what I've been talking about all these years. And just remember, Ma, that the more you work on this, the deeper the understanding and application—just like being back in school, right?? Ha! As if you both ever thought you were <u>done</u> with schooling—whether you are a student or a teacher, you are <u>always</u> learning. I am so proud of you both for all the time, work, effort, and love you have given to me and to Jan—to allow us to express ourselves fully and to reach our highest potentials.

You are the embodiments of <u>great parents</u> and <u>loving friends</u>. Thank you for hanging in with me all these hours, days, months, and years—and not giving up on me. So many of the others I talk with and work with, also coma patients, gather 'round when you guys visit me so that they can also enjoy interacting with people who are willing to take the risk of "being aware and being present."

You want to know what "coma" means to many of us "here"? We see the word as "**Co**operative, **M**utual **A**ssistance." It is far from being a one-way street. So, how can someone in a coma possibly be mutually assisting anyone else in a coopera-tive way when s/he can't even move or commu-nicate?? Well, fasten your seatbelts, Ma and Pa, because the ride is about to get <u>very interesting</u>! *(Debbie's note: Jay is laughing, saying to me, "That ought to get their attention. Think I've made 'em nervous??")*

Okay, here goes . . . human development, evo-lution, and interaction is dependent upon our adapting to life in our physical bodies from the moment we're born (sometimes even before we're born) to the moment we exit the body. Just as an aside, Ma, you know how we're always referring to the law of cause and effect as "karma"? I've given a new spin on that to people here – <u>Kar</u> (as in: car, or vehicle) and <u>ma</u> (as in: mental aware-ness). Get it?? Mental awareness of one's own vehicle! Because our mental awareness, thought patterns and habits, follow us as we go from one vehicle to another. Now, <u>that's</u> something to really chew on. I'm reminding my friends to be careful about what they think, because thought forms *do* affect their vehicles (karma).

Okay, to return to the cooperative, mutual as-sistance idea. It's ironic, really, that people view coma patients (or patients who are incapacitated in other ways) as limited, restricted, communica-tively disabled. We are anything but disabled! It all depends on one's perspective. I know that this will shock and dismay some who read or hear this, but actually, from our vantage point, we are much more "abled" by being in two kinds of real-ity simultaneously. Our physical senses are greatly heightened; yes, even sight, although our eyes may be closed.

How is it that we can "see" without our eyes fully functioning or open? We use other abilities to see a much broader scene, or perspective, than that of limited, physical eyesight. With help and support from both sides (the physical and non-physical realities we occupy), we <u>adapt</u> to our new ways of perceiving. Yes, it is very laborious, time-consuming, and difficult to maneuver in at first, but if our physical forms can be stabilized, our mental (or etheric, whatever you want to term this state of being) adjustments to operating efficiently in both worlds accelerate.

I know, I can already hear the skeptics saying, "Well, so what? If someone's in a coma and can't do anything, what good is it for them to stay around? Why not just let them move on (as in die)? What possible use can someone be if s/he is unconscious? And what about the cost of keeping him/her alive?" We hear and see this all the time. <u>All the time</u>.

We constantly witness families, caregivers, physicians, therapists, administrators expressing grief, loss, anguish, futility, and hopelessness over someone in a coma. People are frequently wondering, "Is there anyone home in this body?" or "We give and give and give, but there's no response back to us (from the coma patient)." Ultimately, "Is it worth keeping this person alive?" Ma and Pa, these are not unusual or cruel thoughts or reactions for anyone to have. This is not a test of one's moral character or intent. It's really a lot simpler than that. What I want to convey is this: How willing are you to have a good look at yourself, how willing are you to take a chance to evolve, expand, and grow beyond your own limitations?

Every time you encounter someone who is or <u>appears to be</u> shut down, you might as well hold a mirror in front of your face. Ask yourself the next time you are with a coma patient or someone of similar circumstance, "What is this person telling me? What aspects of myself are shut down, unable to communicate or interact with others? What aspects of myself am I avoiding dealing with?"

You see, Ma and Pa, by your own courage and love to allow my physical body to stabilize and, indeed, thrive in many ways, we are able to have this communication, or communion, or *co-muni-on(e)* with each other. Yes, it demands great energy and sacrifice on all our parts to keep things going— and, we're all mutually cooperating, benefiting, and very much alive and participating. How else would your lives (or mine) have grown and unfolded if you had given up on me, on us, on our family?

So, where does the <u>assistance</u>, or <u>mutual assistance</u> (the "ma" of co<u>ma</u>) come in? With many of us coma patients, people feel reluctant, uncomfortable, hesitant to simply sit down next to us and just talk gently to us, stroke our hands or arms in a caring way, be loving and sensitive to us. Many think that our minds and senses are locked deeply away in some interior fold of the brain, and that we're oblivious to our external environments. Not so! If anything, we're hypersensitive to most things in our external world, even if we're unable to respond in a demonstrative manner. Temperature is very important, sound is elevated to most of us, and we are especially aware of someone's incoming energy and intention (or lack of).

Mutual assistance to us means that we are key factors and beings in helping those around us in becoming more highly attuned, more highly developed, and more sensitive to themselves, others, and surroundings. By allowing others the opportunity to "sit in the silence" calmly, be receptive, still, spacious, we are creating and allowing a higher level of communication and understanding to be established between us. By encouraging physical, gentle interaction with us, we are fostering a person's ability to get "in touch" with themselves, to seek to understand themselves in a compassionate, fluid way. And ultimately, by being in this coma state, we are giving any and all who interact with us the chance to directly experience union with All-That-Is.

Do you see the stages of evolutionary development for those who are ready, willing, and curious enough to take a chance on life? As you both know, Ma and Pa, it is only in the silence and surrender to our own hearts that we finally find and merge with the One, right? What better teacher or guide can a person have than a coma patient?? And believe me, we are definitely patient!! You might even ask yourself what the difference is between a highly-developed, spiritual master who has taken a vow of silence and a coma patient! Knew that would set you free! Ha, ha.

Do you want to know how we see many of those in physical bodies, what our perceptions are? This is the really **ironic part**—we see many people as if they were patients in a mental facility—all running around in their own private worlds, talking to themselves, wandering aimlessly, trying to make sense of themselves and their worlds. You've said, Ma, that Sai Baba often refers to people on this planet as mad monkeys, right? Well, that's exactly how it looks to others "on the outside." It is crazy (looking). If we can set up communication with even just a few people, get them to be still and quiet enough to receive (rather than constantly transmit), we celebrate!! We are the coma pa-tients with patience helping the mental patients who lack patience.

I cannot adequately describe to you the vast numbers of unseen beings and volunteers who dedicate their energies toward helping the hu-man race. Worlds upon worlds. And yet, in hu-man form, we are so "blind" to this extensive network of aid that we come to think and be-lieve we're on our own, alone, by ourselves. Just realize, Ma and Pa, that this is deliberately (but very thinly) disguised so that we will use every available moment and opportunity to connect (or reconnect), to share, to realize (real eyes, see better) that we are all one, there is no sep-aration, and our interactions with everyone and everything count.

Love is the common "glue" holding all this together. It is the currency we use in the theme park to experience the thrilling-chilling-daring ride. It is the ticket to the first-class seat on the train when we exit the body. It is what makes connection, communication, and Self-realization possible for each and every one of us. Love is actually both the current that drives and sustains us as well as the currency we use to generate meaningful experience.

So, Ma, I would say to your readers, "Enjoy the amusement park while you're here. Take your rides. Make meaningful connections with those around you because they are you. Scream, laugh, cry, shout all you want. And remember to <u>thank the Park Director</u> for your experiences when you exit the park!" Ha, ha.

I love you dearly, Mom and Dad (yes, *Mom and Dad* now, because I want you to know how close I am to both of you). Have already thanked Debbie (don't worry). And, Ma, start gearing up for our next book!! (Jay is laughing and laughing while pointing his finger at Berniece).

Your loving and grateful son,
Love, more love, all the love in the world,
Jay (boy)

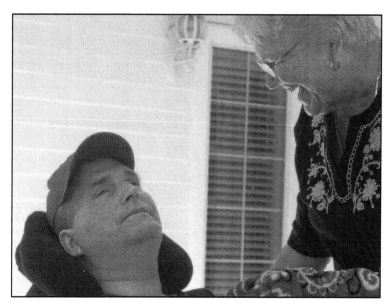

Jay smiling for a photo with Berniece (2010).

You are all the indestructible soul,

the spark of God within; nothing needs to

discourage you. In your dream, you suffer

so much due to fire, floods, insult, loss of

money, and so on. But once you wake up,

you are not affected at all. When these

events happen during the waking state, you

feel afflicted. But let me tell you that from

the state of realization, even the waking

state is equally without validity, It is not the

real "you" that suffers all that. Give up the

delusion that you are this physical entity,

and you become really free.

—Sri Sathya Sai Baba

GLOSSARY

amrita
"nectar of immortality"—the original "nectar of the Gods"; an amber-colored, thick, honey-like liquid that may manifest as a sign of the presence of the Divine

bhajans
devotional songs, devotional singing

Bal Vikas
"the blossoming of the child," or in a broader sense, education that results in "the blossoming of human excellence," through developing virtuous character and morality through the "five human values" of truth, right action, peace, love, and nonviolence; former name of Sai Spiritual Education classes

darshan
the opportunity or blessing of seeing a holy being; seeing divinity

Gayatri mantra
Om bhur bhuvah suvaha, Tat savitur varenyam, Bhargo devasya dhi-mahi, Dhiyo yonah prachodayat. Translation: "We contemplate the

glory of Light illuminating the three worlds: the gross (physical), the subtle (mental), and the causal (spiritual). I am that vivifying power, love, radiant illumination, and divine grace of universal intelligence. We pray for the divine light to illumine all our minds."

Om: The primeval sound

Bhur: the physical world

Bhuvah: the mental world

Suvaha: the celestial, spiritual world

Tat: That; God; the transcendental Paramatma (Supreme Soul)

Savitur: the Sun; refers to Creator, Preserver

Varenyam: most adorable, enchanting

Bhargo: luster, effulgence, radiance, grace, blessings

Devasya: resplendent, supreme Lord

Dheemahi: we meditate upon

Dhiyo: the intellect, understanding

Yo: May this light

Nah: our

Prachodayath: enlighten, guide, inspire

karma   action; results of past action

leela   divine prank or play, divine sport "light meditation" As taught by Sai Baba, one visualizes a flame of light in the heart, spreading that light to all parts of the body—the tongue, the mind, the hands and feet, that all these instruments of thought, word, and action be influenced by the light, to do only good—and then expanding the light outward, infinitely, to include everyone and everything.

lingam   ovoid-shaped object, similar to a stone, that is a mystical symbol that approximates the shape of creation—from the atom, to the solar system, to the universe; a lingam is a symbol of the Formless Absolute coming into form. Sai Baba has created numerous *linga*, some with very unusual properties.

Prasanthi Nilayam   Prasanthi Nilayam, meaning "Abode of Highest Peace," is the name of Sri Sathya Sai Baba's main ashram in Puttaparthi, Andhra Pradesh, India.

sadhana   spiritual discipline, spiritual practice. *Sat* (or *sad*, a variant of the same word root) means truth. A *sadhaka* is a spiritual aspirant or dedicated seeker of spiritual truths; a *sadhu* one who is steady and unwavering in that path.

vibhuti   sacred ash often materialized by Sai Baba; symbolizes the splendor and glory of God that emanates as unending streams of blessings and grace.

ABOUT THE AUTHOR

Berniece Mead is an educator with over 50 years educational experience—30 years in the public schools as an elementary school teacher and over 30 years as a volunteer, teaching and training teachers in character- and values-based education. Since 1994 she has been the USA National Education Coordinator for the Sri Sathya Sai Organization. Internationally, she is a member of the Sri Sathya Sai World Foundation, Education Committee. She travels regularly to all regions of the USA and internationally as a speaker and conductor of teacher trainings in spiritual and values-based education. Her son, **Jay Mead**, the subject and inspiration for *Letters from "J": The Expanded Life of a Coma Patient*, has been in a coma since 1994 and resides in a sub-acute neuro-care facility. Berniece and her husband, Ron, take an active part in Jay's care.

༄

7263258R0